WESTWARD THE WOMEN
An Anthology of Western Stories by Women

WESTWARD THE WOMEN

WOMEN

An Anthology of Western Stories by Women

EDITED BY VICKI PIEKARSKI

DOUBLEDAY & COMPANY, INC.
GARDEN CITY, NEW YORK
1984

ACKNOWLEDGMENTS

Introduction, copyright © 1984 by Vicki Piekarski.

"Mister Death and the Redheaded Woman" by Helen Eustis, copyright © 1950 by the Curtis Publishing Company. First appeared under the title "The Rider on the Pale Horse" in *The Saturday Evening Post*. Reprinted by permission of JCA Literary Agency, Inc.

"Lost Sister" by Dorothy M. Johnson, copyright © 1956 by Dorothy M. Johnson. First appeared in *Cosmopolitan*. Reprinted by permission of McIntosh and Otis, Inc.

"Geranium House" by Peggy Simson Curry, copyright © 1959 by the Western Writers of America. First appeared in *Frontiers West* (Doubleday & Company, 1959). Reprinted by permission of the author.

"The Promise of the Fruit" by Ann Ahlswede, copyright © 1963 by Ann Ahlswede. Reprinted by permission of the author.

"The Deep Valley" by Lucia Moore, copyright © 1963 by Lucia Moore. Reprinted by permission of Gladys Wilkins McCready.

"The Outsider" by Juanita Brooks, copyright © 1982 by Juanita Brooks. First appeared in *Quicksand and Cactus* (Howe Brothers, 1982). Reprinted by permission of Richard Howe.

"Yellow Woman" by Leslie Silko, copyright © 1974 by Leslie Silko. Reprinted by permission of the author.

Library of Congress Cataloging in Publication Data
Main entry under title:
Westward the women.
Contents: Introduction—On the divide/Willa
Cather—The wash-tub mail/Gertrude Atherton—
The last antelope/Mary Austin—[etc.]
1. Western stories. 2. Short stories, American—
Women authors. I. Piekarski, Vicki.
PS648.W4W48   813'.0874'089287

ISBN: 0-385-19187-1
Library of Congress Catalog Card Number 83-25458

CONTENTS

WESTWARD THE WOMEN
An Anthology of Western Stories by Women

INTRODUCTION

In 1934, Nebraska writer Mari Sandoz wrote: ". . . unfortunately I found that the earlier and more exciting portions of pioneer literature have little reference to women outside of dance-hall girls, Indians, and breeds, or those mere bits of icing added for romantic interest in later rehashings of early tales." For all too long, the history of the vast land west of the Mississippi River and the literature inspired by that land have been considered men's domain. It is generally believed that women not only do not read Western fiction but that they do not write it. If a raison d'être must be given for this anthology, let this suffice.

For over five years, while working as coeditor on the *Encyclopedia of Frontier and Western Fiction* (1983), I read Westerns almost exclusively. Eyebrows were raised whenever I purchased a Western, was seen reading a Western, or mentioned the fact that I enjoyed reading Westerns. After the book's publication, in conversations and interviews alike I was constantly asked whether or not women wrote Western fiction.

This regrettable state of affairs is perhaps understandable. The average reader cannot point to any woman writer of Westerns who has met with the success of the men whose books continue to fill the Western sections of bookstores. I admit it. There are no Louisa L'Amours. (But then again, L'Amour is an anomaly, not the rule. Perhaps only Max Brand and Zane Grey—both dead for four decades and so hardly a competitive threat—have rivaled his output.) Furthermore, women are poorly represented in the Western anthologies that are used in classrooms to survey the genre. A number of anthologies do not include women writers at all! But the fact is that women have been writing stories about the West for well over a century. And women both east and west of the Mississippi have been reading their works for the same amount of time. Why, then, do we continue to associate Western fiction writers with husky dark men in cowboy boots, pen in one hand and six-shooter in the other?

Probably one of the main reasons is that the historical experience of settling the West, the "winning of the West," has been until recent years defined as a strictly masculine experience. The publication of Julie Roy Jeffrey's *Frontier Women: The Trans-Mississippi West 1840–1880* (1979), Joanna Stratton's *Pioneer Women: Voices from the Kansas Frontier* (1981), and Sandra L. Myres's *Westering Women and the Frontier Experience 1800–1915* (1982)—all of which survey the lives of ordinary women who settled in the West—have increased our awareness of the fact that our history has been distorted. A glance at any book on the Western frontier prior to 1970 confirms the predominance of the masculine approach to history—with tales of frontiersmen, mountain men, cavalry men, gunfighters, cowboys, ranchmen, Mexican bandidos, and Indian braves, warriors, and chiefs. All of the dramatic sequences woven together to form the tapestry of our Western mythology between book covers and on the screen in both theaters and our homes are male-oriented: walkdowns, barroom brawls, midnight lynchings, and unending Indian attacks. The Western story line must have continuous dramatic action and life-threatening conflict at every turn—and a sharp distinction between hero and villain; it is the cliché-ridden plot line of good versus evil that remains the backbone of Western fiction in the minds of the many who read it. It is this attitude that would confine the Western genre, much as the Indian method of capturing buffalo—the surround—confined the monarch of the Plains centuries back. Surrender is the only possibility when there is no way out, no option.

Westward the Women is the first collection of Western fiction written exclusively by women. The stories in this anthology demonstrate not only that women have written Western stories but also that their perspectives are both original and diverse. It is my hope that this work will show that options *do* abound in the world of Western literature.

Critical works that have examined the history of Western literature have tended to bypass women writers. In fact, although it has been done with male writers, no one has attempted to chart chronologically the history of women's writing about the West. I will attempt, briefly, to fill that void here.

In 1839, the eighth American President, Martin Van Buren, was in office. The Mormons had settled in Illinois to form their community of Nauvoo. The Post Office reported that there were 1,555 newspapers and periodicals in circulation in the United States. Emily Dickinson was nine years old; Samuel Langhorne Clemens was four. *The Prairie* (1826), the latest entry in what would be called James Fenimore Cooper's "Leatherstocking" saga, had been in print for thirteen years. For our purposes, however, 1839 was important because in that year Caroline M. Kirkland's (1801–64) *A New Home—Who'll Follow? or, Glimpses of Western Life* was published under the pseudonym of Mrs. Mary Clavers.

Kirkland was living in what was then the Western frontier, in the present-day town of Pinckney, Michigan. The work, a fictional narrative addressed to friends back East, is about the building of a frontier settlement and is significant historically for a number of reasons. It is the first known work of Western literature to be published in book form by a woman. Secondly, it is often cited as the first work of realism in American literature: it attempted to portray the frontiersman for what he was and what he did, without romanticizing or sentimentalizing him as Cooper and his followers did (and would continue to do). Lastly, the book was the first to show in some detail the day-to-day life of the pioneer woman.

An acquaintance of Kirkland and an admirer of her wit, Edgar Allan Poe, wrote of her in *Literati of New York:* ". . . unquestionably, she is one of our best writers." But by 1900 Kirkland, like Herman Melville, was all but forgotten. Unlike Melville, however, Kirkland never enjoyed a literary revival in the 1920s or at any other time. But already, in this first Western written by a woman—admittedly an autobiographical work closer to nonfiction than fiction—it was clear that women were taking a different approach to this newly developing genre.

The next important writer was Josephine McCrackin (1838–1920), an immigrant from Germany who became involved in the conservation movement in the American West and who published three volumes of short stories. McCrackin specialized in stories set in the Southwest, and wrote vividly about desert scenery and military life. Ambrose Bierce called her work "most interesting." Her stories collected in *Overland Tales* (1877), *Another Juanita* (1893), and *The Woman Who Lost Him* (1913) were sometimes partly autobiographical; they often dealt with heroines fleeing their mates and attempting to make a go of it in a society distrustful of independent women. McCrackin, as Kirkland and so many other subsequent women writers, tended to write about what she knew best: herself and her experience in the West.

Ann Sophia Stephens's (1810–86) place in the history of Western literature is based on the fact that her previously published novella, *Malaeska, The Indian Wife of the White Hunter,* became the first Beadle dime novel in 1860. In terms of the history of women writers, however, Stephens's uniqueness stems from her unusual portrayal of women in nondomestic roles. In her 1858 revision of *Mary Derwent,* the English heroine heads for the American wilderness after a series of tragedies in her home life. Arriving on the frontier, she marries a mixed-blood and becomes leader of his tribe. This story line certainly differs from those by men at that time (and even later), who feared miscegenation and who regarded the rejection of civilization and the flight to the wilderness as exclusively male prerogatives. For many male writers, even today, the West represents a means of repudiating American womanhood.

Mary Hallock Foote (1847–1938) started a successful career as an artist in the East. Her marriage to a civil and mining engineer brought her West in the 1870s, where her art career was expanded to include writing about the places in which she lived: Colorado, Idaho, and California. Her descriptions of the mining frontier were singled out by many critics as rivaling the works of Bret Harte and Mark Twain. Her account of descending into a mine in *The Led Horse Claim* (1883) is both chilling and revelatory. Her books have been less enduring than Harte's and Twain's perhaps because they contain more romance; however, this element was added at the request—ill-advised, in retrospect—of her editors.

In print for a century, *Ramona* (1884) by Helen Hunt Jackson (1830–85) is possibly the best-known book written by an American woman in the nineteenth century. In her novel Jackson attempted to do for the Indians of California what Harriet Beecher Stowe's *Uncle Tom's Cabin* (1852) had done for the Southern blacks. Readers craved romance, however, and it was the Spanish *ricos* and the missions of California that caught their fancy and made the book a publishing success.

A name obscure to all but the collector of rare books is that of Marah Ellis Ryan (1866–1934), whose writing career bridged the turn of the century. Her two most notable books are *Indian Love Letters* (1907) and *The Flute of the Gods* (1909) because of their lyricism and their unusual treatment of the Indians of the Southwest. Ryan's stories often incorporated standardized characters and common literary formulae, but she manipulated these conventional elements to come up with unanticipated plot turns and twists. To an extent, she romanticized the Native American and the Californio, but she did attempt to depict the religious practices and beliefs of the Indian when it was not fashionable to do so. More importantly, she saw the West as a free and invigorating land, particularly for women. In an early work, *Told in the Hills* (1890), reminiscent of Ann Stephens, Ryan portrayed a woman rejecting civilization, preferring the freedom of the frontier.

In the first decade of the twentieth century three significant authors emerged who would continue writing for several decades: B. M. Bower, Mary Austin, and Gertrude Atherton.

Bower (1871–1940), whose career was launched as a successful writer of formulary ranch romances with the publication of *Chip of the Flying U* (1906), had a fine sense of humor, like Kirkland, and her cowboys remain delightful characters. Her women are brave, independent, and interesting—until they fall in love or marry, at which point they invariably become boring. Bower broached any number of social issues in her stories, from divorce to wife beating to the generation gap, but she shied away from treating these issues seriously. In retrospect, it was her wit that probably accounted for most of her success, especially in contrast with her contemporaries, whose outlook in cow country fiction was excessively grim and sober. (Bower's name was sufficiently ambiguous to win both male and female readers. The same can be said of two of today's women writers, Lee Hoffman [1932–] and P. A. Bechko [1950–], who, like Bower, have written comic Westerns. Hoffman, the veteran of the two, has also produced a number of successful serious Westerns, among them *The Valdez Horses* (1967), a book that stands as one of the finest horse stories ever written.)

The literary output of Mary Austin (1868–1934) defies classification. She wrote essays, fiction, belles lettres, nature studies, and plays. Her finest works are *The Land of Little Rain* (1903) and *The Land of Journey's Ending* (1924), about the country and the people of Southern California, Arizona, and New Mexico. These two books contain vignettes of what she saw, heard, and thought about the environment around her, and are, in fact, a rare creative combination of mythology, religion, botany, biology, anthropology, and poetry. Her greatest contribution to Western literature may prove to be her guidelines for the writing of regional stories and her insistence that for the United States to have a truly national literature, Western literature must be recognized as a regional literature worthy of serious attention and consideration. Austin was a human being who truly responded to the land and who sought to capture in precise yet poetic terms the beauty of the lasting elements of that land and its people.

Gertrude Atherton (1857–1948) was an amazingly prolific writer whose work ranged over a great many subjects and settings. It was Atherton's intention to study the history of California and the development of the new California woman in a series of eighteen novels, beginning with her book *The Splendid Idle Forties* (1902). Atherton's heroines seek a new identity; they question their traditional roles and the expectations carved out for them because of their background, class, and ancestry. Atherton was an uneven writer, but she attempted to do something totally original with Western regional fiction. Her female creations were intelligent and aware of their sexuality—a rare combination in Western fiction.

Although Willa Cather (1873–1947) began writing before the advent of the twentieth century, her deserved success came in 1913 with the publication of *O Pioneers!*, followed five years later by *My Ántonia*. With these two enduring novels and later with *Death Comes for the Archbishop* (1927), Cather made Westering seem a universal human experience, and in the process brought frontier literature to new heights of critical and popular esteem. These books not only made immigrants fascinating grist for the writer's mill, but also proved that female characters were capable of carrying a story without the interference of a sentimental romance. It was the love of the land, such as Mary Austin had prescribed, that made these books such lasting works of literature.

The same year that Cather's *O Pioneers!* was published,

Honoré Willsie Morrow's (1880–1940) *The Heart of the Desert* appeared. In this book, as in her later *The Enchanted Canyon* (1921), Morrow advocated desert and forest reclamation. Her novels were set in various locales of the West. She popularized historical treatment of the Western in *We Must March: A Novel of the Winning of Oregon* (1925), before such treatments became popular in the Thirties.

The pioneering efforts of the immigrant in Iowa—with emphasis on those from Germany—was the focus of Midwestern writer Ruth Suckow (1892–1960). She began her writing career in the Twenties. Suckow was classed as a realist and commonly dealt with conflicts between the generations in a new land. In *The Folks* (1934), her longest and finest novel, she explored the theme of continuity versus change.

The Thirties saw the first of the "Little House" books by Laura Ingalls Wilder (1867–1957): *The Little House in the Big Woods* (1932) and *Little House on the Prairie* (1935). These books, written for children, followed the tradition of Cather and Suckow in that they dealt with the day-to-day experiences of pioneer families. Wilder stressed the strength women needed to survive on the Great Plains. Rose Wilder Lane (1887–1968), Laura's daughter, began writing regional novels set in Missouri and Arkansas in the mid-Twenties. Her later stories about pioneer life lack the simplicity of Wilder's books, although they are authentic re-creations.

Cather, Suckow, Wilder, and Lane helped to bring legitimacy to the pioneer story about those immigrants who settled in the new land west of the Mississippi.

Over the years, Edna Ferber's (1885–1968) novels have frequently been dismissed as sentimental and escapist. But many of her books, such as *Cimarron* (1930), seem simply to have been misunderstood. Ferber intended *Cimarron*, a novel of the Oklahoma land rush of 1889, to be a "malevolent picture of what is known as American womanhood and American sentimentality." She set each of her novels in a different state, and in many cases she angered the inhabitants of those particular areas—Texans, for example, didn't take very kindly to *Giant* (1952). Ferber strongly believed that men are dreamers, women are doers; and in her books women are shown as indispensable to the building of communities.

Texans were also outraged earlier when Dorothy Scarborough (1877–1935) anonymously published *The Wind* (1925); her name was added later to subsequent editions. *The Wind* was unique in its completely pessimistic interpretation of the effect frontier life had on a young woman from the East. This powerfully written psychological study in defeat was significant because it showed that the land, the impoverished lifestyle, and the hot, dry climate could destroy a person ill-prepared to meet the challenges of Western life.

The literary focus of Mari Sandoz (1896–1966) was the Great Plains. The magnum opus of the Sandoz canon is the Trans-Missouri series, a six-volume history of the Great Plains that includes *Old Jules* (1935), a biography of the author's father and a classic work on homesteaders. Sandoz wrote eight novels about the inhabitants of the Great Plains region, whites and Indians alike. Her novel *Miss Morissa: Doctor of the Gold Trail* (1955) is one of the best fictional accounts we have of a woman professional on the frontier. Carl Sandburg wrote of her: "The very rare and superbly American Mari Sandoz. Some of her books will be standing and in use when the best sellers of the period are in the dustbins of oblivion."

Virginia Sorensen (1912–) is a native of Utah. Her first novel, *A Little Lower Than the Angels* (1942), is about the Mormons in Nauvoo, Illinois. Her later books explore the effects of a predominantly male environment on women and the problems of rootlessness, and these works constitute her finest achievement.

Perhaps the best known of all modern-day women Western writers is Dorothy M. Johnson (1905–). Her reputation as one of the genre's best short story writers rests on two collections of Westerns: *Indian Country* (1953) and *The Hanging Tree* (1957). The veteran Western writer Jack Schaefer has summed up Johnson's work succinctly: "Here is no glamorizing, no romantic gilding, of settlers or of Indians. Here is something finer and more gripping, the honest portrayal of good and bad, of strength and frailty, of the admirable and the contemptible, in both white settlements and Indian villages." Johnson ranks as "one of the boys," and almost every Western anthology contains at least one of her stories. Although she has continued writing—including a number of novels about Indians written from the female point of view—none of her more recent work has received the acclaim of her stories of the Fifties.

Aside from P. A. Bechko and Lee Hoffman, there are few women writing Westerns today whose output is as regular and prolific as that of the leading male authors—perhaps because women tend to write the kind of historical fiction that takes painstaking research and years of work. Writers such as Dorothy Gardiner (1894–), who wrote *The Golden Lady* (1936), one of the finest novels on the mining frontier I have ever read, often produce only two or three Western books. And many women writers have added new dimensions to the field of Western literature, and then (to use Tillie Olsen's term) have become "silent": Gwen Bristow (1903–80), Jane Barry (1925–), Lucia Moore (1887–1983), Ann Ahlswede (1928–), and Marilyn Durham (1930–), among others. In the Eighties, Anna Lee Waldo and Lucia St. Clair Robson have written massive tomes on historical women: Sacajawea and Cynthia Ann Parker. Will we hear more from them? Or will they too fall silent?

Women have helped refine, reshape, and redefine the form of the historical novel to embrace wider frontiers. In their concern with history they have begun to unravel the tightly woven mythos of the American West. They have tackled social issues that others would have preferred to ignore. They have served as the conscience of our history by questioning actions and policies of the past. Treated as a minority themselves, women have often been sympathetic to the peoples native to this land. They have asked what the frontier offered and what it denied. And they have examined and explored the effects that the frontier had on women's constant search for a clearer identity. Women have not been afraid to break away from stereotypes, for they have understood from the very beginning that the frontier was both a masculine and a feminine experience—a *human* experience, for better or worse.

The twelve stories in this volume represent seventy-nine years of women's writing about the West. What the reader may find most impressive about these stories is their wide variety of Western subjects. Here are stories about a white's captivity among the Indians; the effects of the Civil War; Basque sheepherders; the hardships of pioneer life; drought; the cultural clash between the Anglos and the Spanish and Native Americans; the lack of professionals on the frontier; Mormons, squawmen, immigrants; and Indian mythology. And these stories deal, too, with daily aspects of the human condition that extend beyond the borders of the American West: love, marriage, loneliness, friendship, the generation gap, tradition, and death.

The stories are not confined to any one region of the West, but take in California ("The Wash-Tub Mail" and "The Last Antelope"), the Great Plains ("On the Divide" and "The Vine"), Utah ("The Outsider"), the Pacific Northwest ("The Deep Valley"), the Southwest ("Yellow Woman"), and Montana ("When the Cook Fell Ill"). Wherever the story may be set, the author enriches the reader's awareness of the varying landscape of the Western terrain. From the beginning, women have been aware that the *land* of the West is an integral part of a Western story.

My reason for assembling this anthology was to present a representative selection of Western stories by women that would correct the impression that women have been only marginal contributors to the genre. There is nothing marginal about their unique literary tradition. Each of these stories is a clear testimony of its author's love and respect for the American West, its history and its people. Long after the passing of the frontier, the Westering experience has continued to inspire women and their creative imaginations.

Vicki Piekarski

Portland, Oregon

ON THE DIVIDE
WILLA CATHER (1873–1947)

Cather was born near Winchester, Virginia. At an early age, she and her family moved to Nebraska, the region Cather would one day use as her literary cynosure. A little-known and grim story, "On the Divide" is representative of Cather's very early work. It appeared in the *Overland* in January 1896. The plot of the story is less interesting than Cather's description of the protagonist, Canute Canuteson, a solitary Norwegian giant, and his environs. Lena Yensen, the object of Canute's desire, is an early, undeveloped prototype of Lena Lingard in *My Ántonia* (1918). Cather's artistry—subtle, simple, and inspired by the land—spoke to many people, including such authors as Norway's Sigrid Undset, who kept a picture of Cather on her writing table.

Near Rattlesnake Creek, on the side of a little draw stood Canute's shanty. North, east, south, stretched the level Nebraska plain of long rust-red grass that undulated constantly in the wind. To the west the ground was broken and rough, and a narrow strip of timber wound along the turbid, muddy little stream that had scarcely ambition enough to crawl over its black bottom. If it had not been for the few stunted cottonwoods and elms that grew along its banks, Canute would have shot himself years ago. The Norwegians are a timber-loving people, and if there is even a turtle pond with a few plum bushes around it they seem irresistibly drawn toward it.

As to the shanty itself, Canute had built it without aid of any kind, for when he first squatted along the banks of Rattle-

snake Creek there was not a human being within twenty
miles. It was built of logs split in halves, the chinks stopped
with mud and plaster. The roof was covered with earth and
was supported by one gigantic beam curved in the shape of a
round arch. It was almost impossible that any tree had ever
grown in that shape. The Norwegians used to say that Canute
had taken the log across his knee and bent it into the shape he
wished. There were two rooms, or rather there was one room
with a partition made of ash saplings interwoven and bound
together like big straw basket work. In one corner there was
a cook stove, rusted and broken. In the other a bed made of
unplaned planks and poles. It was fully eight feet long, and
upon it was a heap of dark bed clothing. There was a chair
and a bench of colossal proportions. There was an ordinary
kitchen cupboard with a few cracked dirty dishes in it, and
beside it on a tall box a tin washbasin. Under the bed was a
pile of pint flasks, some broken, some whole, all empty. On
the wood box lay a pair of shoes of almost incredible dimensions. On the wall hung a saddle, a gun, and some ragged
clothing, conspicuous among which was a suit of dark cloth,
apparently new, with a paper collar carefully wrapped in a
red silk handkerchief and pinned to the sleeve. Over the
door hung a wolf and a badger skin, and on the door itself a
brace of thirty or forty snake skins whose noisy tails rattled
ominously every time it opened. The strangest things in the
shanty were the wide window sills. At first glance they looked
as though they had been ruthlessly hacked and mutilated
with a hatchet, but on closer inspection all the notches and
holes in the wood took form and shape. There seemed to be a
series of pictures. They were, in a rough way, artistic, but the
figures were heavy and labored, as though they had been cut
very slowly and with very awkward instruments. There were
men plowing with little horned imps sitting on their shoulders and on their horses' heads. There were men praying
with a skull hanging over their heads and little demons behind them mocking their attitudes. There were men fighting
with big serpents, and skeletons dancing together. All about

these pictures were blooming vines and foliage such as never grew in this world, and coiled among the branches of the vines there was always the scaly body of a serpent, and behind every flower there was a serpent's head. It was a veritable Dance of Death by one who had felt its sting. In the wood box lay some boards, and every inch of them was cut up in the same manner. Sometimes the work was very rude and careless, and looked as though the hand of the workman had trembled. It would sometimes have been hard to distinguish the men from their evil geniuses but for one fact, the men were always grave and were either toiling or praying, while the devils were always smiling and dancing. Several of these boards had been split for kindling and it was evident that the artist did not value his work highly.

It was the first day of winter on the Divide. Canute stumbled into his shanty carrying a basket of cobs, and after filling the stove, sat down on a stool and crouched his seven-foot frame over the fire, staring drearily out of the window at the wide gray sky. He knew by heart every individual clump of bunch grass in the miles of red shaggy prairie that stretched before his cabin. He knew it in all the deceitful loveliness of its early summer, in all the bitter barrenness of its autumn. He had seen it smitten by all the plagues of Egypt. He had seen it parched by drought, and sogged by rain, beaten by hail, and swept by fire, and in the grasshopper years he had seen it eaten as bare and clean as bones that the vultures have left. After the great fires he had seen it stretch for miles and miles, black and smoking as the floor of hell.

He rose slowly and crossed the room, dragging his big feet heavily as though they were burdens to him. He looked out of the window into the hog corral and saw the pigs burying themselves in the straw before the shed. The leaden gray clouds were beginning to spill themselves, and the snow flakes were settling down over the white leprous patches of frozen earth where the hogs had gnawed even the sod away. He shuddered and began to walk, trampling heavily with his ungainly feet. He was the wreck of ten winters on the Divide and he knew what that meant. Men fear the winters of the Divide as a child fears night or as men in the North Seas fear the still dark cold of the polar twilight.

His eyes fell upon his gun, and he took it down from the wall and looked it over. He sat down on the edge of his bed and held the barrel towards his face, letting his forehead rest upon it, and laid his finger on the trigger. He was perfectly calm, there was neither passion nor despair in his face, but the thoughtful look of a man who is considering. Presently he laid down the gun, and reaching into the cupboard, drew out a pint bottle of raw white alcohol. Lifting it to his lips, he drank greedily. He washed his face in the tin basin and combed his rough hair and shaggy blond beard. Then he stood in uncertainty before the suit of dark clothes that hung on the wall. For the fiftieth time he took them in his hands and tried to summon courage to put them on. He took the paper collar that was pinned to the sleeve of the coat and cautiously slipped it under his rough beard, looking with timid expectancy into the cracked, splashed glass that hung over the bench. With a short laugh he threw it down on the bed, and pulling on his old black hat, he went out, striking off across the level.

It was a physical necessity for him to get away from his cabin once in a while. He had been there for ten years, digging and plowing and sowing, and reaping what little the hail and the hot winds and the frosts left him to reap. Insanity and suicide are very common things on the Divide. They come on like an epidemic in the hot wind season. Those scorching dusty winds that blow up over the bluffs from Kansas seem to dry up the blood in men's veins as they do the sap in the corn leaves. Whenever the yellow scorch creeps down over the tender inside leaves about the ear, then the coroners prepare for active duty; for the oil of the country is burned out and it does not take long for the flame to eat up the wick. It causes no great sensation there when a Dane is found swinging to his own windmill tower, and most of the

Poles after they have become too careless and discouraged to shave themselves keep their razors to cut their throats with.

It may be that the next generation on the Divide will be very happy, but the present one came too late in life. It is useless for men that have cut hemlocks among the mountains of Sweden for forty years to try to be happy in a country as flat and gray and as naked as the sea. It is not easy for men that have spent their youth fishing in the Northern seas to be content with following a plow, and men that have served in the Austrian army hate hard work and coarse clothing on the loneliness of the plains, and long for marches and excitement and tavern company and pretty barmaids. After a man has passed his fortieth birthday it is not easy for him to change the habits and conditions of his life. Most men bring with them to the Divide only the dregs of the lives that they have squandered in other lands and among other peoples.

Canute Canuteson was as mad as any of them, but his madness did not take the form of suicide or religion but of alcohol. He had always taken liquor when he wanted it, as all Norwegians do, but after his first year of solitary life he settled down to it steadily. He exhausted whisky after a while, and went to alcohol, because its effects were speedier and surer. He was a big man and with a terrible amount of resistant force, and it took a great deal of alcohol even to move him. After nine years of drinking, the quantities he could take would seem fabulous to an ordinary drinking man. He never let it interfere with his work, he generally drank at night and on Sundays. Every night, as soon as his chores were done, he began to drink. While he was able to sit up he would play on his mouth harp or hack away at his window sills with his jack knife. When the liquor went to his head he would lie down on his bed and stare out of the window until he went to sleep. He drank alone and in solitude not for pleasure or good cheer, but to forget the awful loneliness and level of the Divide. Milton made a sad blunder when he put mountains in hell. Mountains postulate faith and aspiration. All mountain peoples are religious. It was the cities of the plains that, because of their utter lack of spirituality and the mad caprice of their vice, were cursed by God.

Alcohol is perfectly consistent in its effects upon man. Drunkenness is merely an exaggeration. A foolish man drunk becomes maudlin; a bloody man, vicious; a coarse man, vulgar. Canute was none of these, but he was morose and gloomy, and liquor took him through all the hells of Dante. As he lay on his giant's bed all the horrors of this world and every other were laid bare to his chilled senses. He was a man who knew no joy, a man who toiled in silence and bitterness. The skull and the serpent were always before him, the symbols of eternal futileness and of eternal hate.

When the first Norwegians near enough to be called neighbors came, Canute rejoiced, and planned to escape from his bosom vice. But he was not a social man by nature and had not the power of drawing out the social side of other people. His new neighbors rather feared him because of his great strength and size, his silence and his lowering brows. Perhaps, too, they knew that he was mad, mad from the eternal treachery of the plains, which every spring stretch green and rustle with the promises of Eden, showing long grassy lagoons full of clear water and cattle whose hoofs are stained with wild roses. Before autumn the lagoons are dried up, and the ground is burnt dry and hard until it blisters and cracks open.

So instead of becoming a friend and neighbor to the men that settled about him, Canute became a mystery and a terror. They told awful stories of his size and strength and of the alcohol he drank. They said that one night, when he went out to see to his horses just before he went to bed, his steps were unsteady and the rotten planks of the floor gave way and threw him behind the feet of a fiery young stallion. His foot was caught fast in the floor, and the nervous horse began kicking frantically. When Canute felt the blood trickling down into his eyes from a scalp wound in his head, he roused himself from his kingly indifference, and with the quiet stoical courage of a drunken man leaned forward and wound his

arms about the horse's hind legs and held them against his
breast with crushing embrace. All through the darkness and
cold of the night he lay there, matching strength against
strength. When little Jim Peterson went over the next morning at four o'clock to go with him to the Blue to cut wood, he
found him so, and the horse was on its fore knees, trembling
and whinnying with fear. This is the story the Norwegians
tell of him, and if it is true it is no wonder that they feared and
hated this Holder of the Heels of Horses.

One spring there moved to the next "eighty" a family that
made a great change in Canute's life. Ole Yensen was too
drunk most of the time to be afraid of any one, and his wife
Mary was too garrulous to be afraid of any one who listened
to her talk, and Lena, their pretty daughter, was not afraid of
man nor devil. So it came about that Canute went over to
take his alcohol with Ole oftener than he took it alone. After a
while the report spread that he was going to marry Yensen's
daughter, and the Norwegian girls began to tease Lena about
the great bear she was going to keep house for. No one could
quite see how the affair had come about, for Canute's tactics
of courtship were somewhat peculiar. He apparently never
spoke to her at all: he would sit for hours with Mary chattering on one side of him and Ole drinking on the other and
watch Lena at her work. She teased him, and threw flour in
his face and put vinegar in his coffee, but he took her rough
jokes with silent wonder, never even smiling. He took her to
church occasionally, but the most watchful and curious people never saw him speak to her. He would sit staring at her
while she giggled and flirted with the other men.

Next spring Mary Lee went to town to work in a steam
laundry. She came home every Sunday, and always ran across
to Yensens to startle Lena with stories of ten cent theaters,
firemen's dances, and all the other esthetic delights of metro-
politan life. In a few weeks Lena's head was completely
turned, and she gave her father no rest until he let her go to
town to seek her fortune at the ironing board. From the time
she came home on her first visit she began to treat Canute

with contempt. She had bought a plush cloak and kid gloves, had her clothes made by the dress-maker, and assumed airs and graces that made the other women of the neighborhood cordially detest her. She generally brought with her a young man from town who waxed his mustache and wore a red necktie, and she did not even introduce him to Canute.

The neighbors teased Canute a good deal until he knocked one of them down. He gave no sign of suffering from her neglect except that he drank more and avoided the other Norwegians more carefully than ever. He lay around in his den and no one knew what he felt or thought, but little Jim Peterson, who had seen him glowering at Lena in church one Sunday when she was there with the town man, said that he would not give an acre of his wheat for Lena's life or the town chap's either; and Jim's wheat was so wondrously worthless that the statement was an exceedingly strong one.

Canute had bought a new suit of clothes that looked as nearly like the town man's as possible. They had cost him half a millet crop; for tailors are not accustomed to fitting giants and they charge for it. He had hung those clothes in his shanty two months ago and had never put them on, partly from fear of ridicule, partly from discouragement, and partly because there was something in his own soul that revolted at the littleness of the device.

Lena was at home just at this time. Work was slack in the laundry and Mary had not been well, so Lena stayed at home, glad enough to get an opportunity to torment Canute once more.

She was washing in the side kitchen, singing loudly as she worked. Mary was on her knees, blacking the stove and scolding violently about the young man who was coming out from town that night. The young man had committed the fatal error of laughing at Mary's ceaseless babble and had never been forgiven.

"He is no good, and you will come to a bad end by running with him! I do not see why a daughter of mine should act so. I do not see why the Lord should visit such a punishment upon me as to give me such a daughter. There are plenty of good men you can marry."

Lena tossed her head and answered curtly, "I don't happen to want to marry any man right away, and so long as Dick dresses nice and has plenty of money to spend, there is no harm in my going with him."

"Money to spend? Yes, and that is all he does with it I'll be bound. You think it very fine now, but you will change your tune when you have been married five years and see your children running naked and your cupboard empty. Did Anne Hermanson come to any good end by marrying a town man?"

"I don't know anything about Anne Hermanson, but I know any of the laundry girls would have Dick quick enough if they could get him."

"Yes, and a nice lot of store clothes huzzies you are too. Now there is Canuteson who has an 'eighty' proved up and fifty head of cattle and—"

"And hair that ain't been cut since he was a baby, and a big dirty beard, and he wears overalls on Sundays, and drinks like a pig. Besides he will keep. I can have all the fun I want, and when I am old and ugly like you he can have me and take care of me. The Lord knows there ain't nobody else going to marry him."

Canute drew his hand back from the latch as though it were red hot. He was not the kind of man to make a good eavesdropper, and he wished he had knocked sooner. He pulled himself together and struck the door like a battering ram. Mary jumped and opened it with a screech.

"God! Canute, how you scared us! I thought it was crazy Lou—he has been tearing around the neighborhood trying to convert folks. I am afraid as death of him. He ought to be sent off, I think. He is just as liable as not to kill us all, or burn the barn, or poison the dogs. He has been worrying even the poor minister to death, and he laid up with the rheumatism, too! Did you notice that he was too sick to preach last Sunday? But don't stand there in the cold, come in. Yensen isn't here, but he just went over to Sorenson's for the mail; he won't be gone long. Walk right in the other room and sit down."

Canute followed her, looking steadily in front of him and not noticing Lena as he passed her. But Lena's vanity would not allow him to pass unmolested. She took the wet sheet she was wringing out and cracked him across the face with it, and ran giggling to the other side of the room. The blow stung his cheeks and the soapy water flew in his eyes, and he involuntarily began rubbing them with his hands. Lena giggled with delight at his discomfiture, and the wrath in Canute's face grew blacker than ever. A big man humiliated is vastly more undignified than a little one. He forgot the sting of his face in the bitter consciousness that he had made a fool of himself. He stumbled blindly into the living room, knocking his head against the door jamb because he forgot to stoop. He dropped into a chair behind the stove, thrusting his big feet back helplessly on either side of him.

Ole was a long time in coming, and Canute sat there, still and silent, with his hands clenched on his knees, and the skin of his face seemed to have shriveled up into little wrinkles that trembled when he lowered his brows. His life had been one long lethargy of solitude and alcohol, but now he was awakening, and it was as when the dumb stagnant heat of summer breaks out into thunder.

When Ole came staggering in, heavy with liquor, Canute rose at once.

"Yensen," he said quietly, "I have come to see if you will let me marry your daughter today."

"Today!" gasped Ole.

"Yes, I will not wait until tomorrow. I am tired of living alone."

Ole braced his staggering knees against the bedstead, and stammered eloquently: "Do you think I will marry my daughter to a drunkard? a man who drinks raw alcohol? a man who sleeps with rattlesnakes? Get out of my house or I

will kick you out for your impudence." And Ole began looking anxiously for his feet.

Canute answered not a word, but he put on his hat and
went out into the kitchen. He went up to Lena and said
without looking at her, "Get your things on and come with
me!"

The tones of his voice startled her, and she said angrily,
dropping the soap, "Are you drunk?"

"If you do not come with me, I will take you—you had
better come," said Canute quietly.

She lifted a sheet to strike him, but he caught her arm
roughly and wrenched the sheet from her. He turned to the
wall and took down a hood and shawl that hung there, and
began wrapping her up. Lena scratched and fought like a
wild thing. Ole stood in the door, cursing, and Mary howled
and screeched at the top of her voice. As for Canute, he lifted
the girl in his arms and went out of the house. She kicked and
struggled, but the helpless wailing of Mary and Ole soon died
away in the distance, and her face was held down tightly on
Canute's shoulder so that she could not see whither he was
taking her. She was conscious only of the north wind
whistling in her ears, and of rapid steady motion and of a
great breast that heaved beneath her in quick irregular
breaths. The harder she struggled the tighter those iron arms
that had held the heels of horses crushed about her, until she
felt as if they would crush the breath from her, and lay still
with fear. Canute was striding across the level fields at a pace
at which man never went before, drawing the stinging north
winds into his lungs in great gulps. He walked with his eyes
half closed and looking straight in front of him, only lowering
them when he bent his head to blow away the snow flakes
that settled on her hair. So it was that Canute took her to his
home, even as his bearded barbarian ancestors took the fair
frivolous women of the South in their hairy arms and bore
them down to their war ships. For ever and anon the soul
becomes weary of the conventions that are not of it, and with
a single stroke shatters the civilized lies with which it is

unable to cope, and the strong arm reaches out and takes by force what it cannot win by cunning.

When Canute reached his shanty he placed the girl upon a chair, where she sat sobbing. He stayed only a few minutes. He filled the stove with wood and lit the lamp, drank a huge swallow of alcohol and put the bottle in his pocket. He paused a moment, staring heavily at the weeping girl, then he went off and locked the door and disappeared in the gathering gloom of the night.

Wrapped in flannels and soaked with turpentine, the little Norwegian preacher sat reading his Bible, when he heard a thundering knock at his door, and Canute entered, covered with snow and his beard frozen fast to his coat.

"Come in, Canute, you must be frozen," said the little man, shoving a chair towards his visitor.

Canute remained standing with his hat on and said quietly, "I want you to come over to my house tonight to marry me to Lena Yensen."

"Have you got a license, Canute?"

"No, I don't want a license. I want to be married."

"But I can't marry you without a license, man. It would not be legal."

A dangerous light came in the big Norwegian's eye. "I want you to come over to my house to marry me to Lena Yensen."

"No, I can't, it would kill an ox to go out in a storm like this, and my rheumatism is bad tonight."

"Then if you will not go I must take you," said Canute with a sigh.

He took down the preacher's bearskin coat and bade him put it on while he hitched up his buggy. He went out and closed the door softly after him. Presently he returned and found the frightened minister crouching before the fire with his coat lying beside him. Canute helped him put it on and gently wrapped his head in his big muffler. Then he picked him up and carried him out and placed him in his buggy. As he tucked the buffalo robes around him he said: "Your horse is old, he might flounder or lose his way in this storm. I will lead him."

The minister took the reins feebly in his hands and sat shivering with the cold. Sometimes when there was a lull in the wind, he could see the horse struggling through the snow with the man plodding steadily beside him. Again the blowing snow would hide them from him altogether. He had no idea where they were or what direction they were going. He felt as though he were being whirled away in the heart of the storm, and he said all the prayers he knew. But at last the long four miles were over, and Canute set him down in the snow while he unlocked the door. He saw the bride sitting by the fire with her eyes red and swollen as though she had been weeping. Canute placed a huge chair for him, and said roughly,—

"Warm yourself."

Lena began to cry and moan afresh, begging the minister to take her home. He looked helplessly at Canute. Canute said simply, "If you are warm now, you can marry us."

"My daughter, do you take this step of your own free will?" asked the minister in a trembling voice.

"No, sir, I don't, and it is disgraceful he should force me into it! I won't marry him."

"Then Canute, I cannot marry you," said the minister, standing as straight as his rheumatic limbs would let him.

"Are you ready to marry us now, sir?" said Canute, laying one iron hand on his stooped shoulder. The little preacher was a good man, but like most men of weak body he was a coward and had a horror of physical suffering, although he had known so much of it. So with many qualms of conscience he began to repeat the marriage service. Lena sat sullenly in her chair, staring at the fire. Canute stood beside her, listening with his head bent reverently and his hands folded on his breast. When the little man had prayed and said amen, Canute began bundling him up again.

"I will take you home, now," he said as he carried him out and placed him in his buggy, and started off with him through the fury of the storm, floundering among the snow drifts that brought even the giant himself to his knees.

After she was left alone, Lena soon ceased weeping. She was not of a particularly sensitive temperament, and had little pride beyond that of vanity. After the first bitter anger wore itself out, she felt nothing more than a healthy sense of humiliation and defeat. She had no inclination to run away, for she was married now, and in her eyes that was final and all rebellion was useless. She knew nothing about a license, but she knew that a preacher married folks. She consoled herself by thinking that she had always intended to marry Canute someday, anyway.

She grew tired of crying and looking into the fire, so she got up and began to look about her. She had heard queer tales about the inside of Canute's shanty, and her curiosity soon got the better of her rage. One of the first things she noticed was the new black suit of clothes hanging on the wall. She was dull, but it did not take a vain woman long to interpret anything so decidedly flattering, and she was pleased in spite of herself. As she looked through the cupboard, the general air of neglect and discomfort made her pity the man who lived there.

"Poor fellow, no wonder he wants to get married to get somebody to wash up his dishes. Batchin's pretty hard on a man."

It is easy to pity when once one's vanity has been tickled. She looked at the window sill and gave a little shudder and wondered if the man were crazy. Then she sat down again and sat a long time wondering what her Dick and Ole would do.

"It is queer Dick didn't come right over after me. He surely came, for he would have left town before the storm began and he might just as well come right on as go back. If he'd hurried he would have gotten here before the preacher came. I suppose he was afraid to come, for he knew Canuteson would pound him to jelly, the coward!" Her eyes flashed angrily.

The weary hours wore on and Lena began to grow horribly lonesome. It was an uncanny night and this was an uncanny place to be in. She could hear the coyotes howling hungrily a little way from the cabin, and more terrible still were all the unknown noises of the storm. She remembered the tales they told of the big log overhead and she was afraid of those snaky things on the window sills. She remembered the man who had been killed in the draw, and she wondered what she would do if she saw crazy Lou's white face glaring into the window. The rattling of the door became unbearable, she thought the latch must be loose and took the lamp to look at it. Then for the first time she saw the ugly brown snake skins whose death rattle sounded every time the wind jarred the door.

"Canute, Canute!" she screamed in terror.

Outside the door she heard a heavy sound as of a big dog getting up and shaking himself. The door opened and Canute stood before her, white as a snow drift.

"What is it?" he asked kindly.

"I am cold," she faltered.

He went out and got an armful of wood and a basket of cobs and filled the stove. Then he went out and lay in the snow before the door. Presently he heard her calling again.

"What is it?" he said, sitting up.

"I'm so lonesome, I'm afraid to stay in here all alone."

"I will go over and get your mother." And he got up.

"She won't come."

"I'll bring her," said Canute grimly.

"No, no. I don't want her, she will scold all the time."

"Well, I will bring your father."

She spoke again and it seemed as though her mouth was close up to the key-hole. She spoke lower than he had ever heard her speak before, so low that he had to put his ear up to the lock to hear her.

"I don't want him either, Canute,—I'd rather have you."

For a moment she heard no noise at all, then something like a groan. With a cry of fear she opened the door, and saw Canute stretched in the snow at her feet, his face in his hands, sobbing on the door step.

THE WASH-TUB MAIL

GERTRUDE ATHERTON
(1857–1948)

Gertrude Atherton wrote best about her native state, California. "The Wash-Tub Mail" is taken from her short story collection *The Splendid Idle Forties* (1902), about which Jack Schaefer once wrote: ". . . there are some flashes of gold in the pages." This story is distinguished by its marvelous thumbnail portraits of the Spanish washerwomen who meet to gossip about the events around Monterey. The story covers a period of almost twenty years, and the reader learns of the slow but certain takeover of California by the Anglo-Americans through Atherton's expert narration of a doomed romance between the conquered La Tulita, an old-world, aristocratic young woman, and the conqueror, an American lieutenant.

PART I

"Mariquita! Thou good-for-nothing, thou art wringing that smock in pieces! Thy señora will beat thee! Holy heaven, but it is hot!"

"For that reason I hurry, old Faquita. Were I as slow as thou, I should cook in my own tallow."

"Aha, thou art very clever! But I have no wish to go back to the rancho and wash for the cooks. Ay, yi! I wonder will La Tulita ever give me her bridal clothes to wash. I have no faith that little flirt will marry the Señor Don Ramon Garcia. He did not well to leave Monterey until after the wedding. And to think—Ay! yi!"

"Thou hast a big letter for the wash-tub mail, Faquita."

"Aha, my Francesca, thou hast interest! I thought thou wast thinking only of the bandits."

Francesca, who was holding a plunging child between her knees, actively inspecting its head, grunted but did not look up, and the oracle of the wash-tubs, provokingly, with slow movements of her knotted coffee-colored arms, flapped a dainty skirt, half-covered with drawn work, before she condescended to speak further.

Twenty women or more, young and old, dark as pine cones, stooped or sat, knelt or stood, about deep stone tubs sunken in the ground at the foot of a hill on the outskirts of Monterey. The pines cast heavy shadows on the long slope above them, but the sun was overhead. The little white town looked lifeless under its baking red tiles, at this hour of siesta. On the blue bay rode a warship flying the American colors. The atmosphere was so clear, the view so uninterrupted, that the younger women fancied they could read the name on the prow: the town was on the right; between the bay and the tubs lay only the meadow, the road, the lake, and the marsh. A few yards farther down the road rose a hill where white slabs and crosses gleamed beneath the trees. The roar of the surf came refreshingly to their hot ears. It leaped angrily, they fancied, to the old fort on the hill where men in the uniform of the United States moved about with unsleeping vigilance. It was the year 1847. The Americans had come and conquered. War was over, but the invaders guarded their new possessions.

The women about the tubs still bitterly protested against the downfall of California, still took an absorbing interest in all matters, domestic, social, and political. For those old women with grizzled locks escaping from a cotton handkerchief wound bandwise about their heads, their ample forms untrammeled by the flowing garment of calico, those girls in bright skirts and white short-sleeved smock and young hair braided, knew all the news of the country, past and to come, many hours in advance of the dons and doñas whose linen they washed in the great stone tubs: the Indians, domestic and roving, were their faithful friends.

"Sainted Mary, but thou art more slow than a gentleman that walks!" cried Mariquita, an impatient-looking girl. "Read us the letter. La Tulita is the prettiest girl in Monterey now that the Señorita Ysabel Herrera lies beneath the rocks, and Benicia Ortega has died of her childing. But she is a flirt —that Tulita! Four of the Gringos are under her little slipper this year, and she turn over the face and roll in the dirt. But Don Ramon, so handsome, so rich—surely she will marry him."

Faquita shook her head slowly and wisely. "There—come —yesterday—from—the—South—a—young—lieutenant— of—America." She paused a moment, then proceeded lei- surely, though less provokingly. "He come over the great American deserts with General Kearny last year and help our men to eat the dust in San Diego. He come only yesterday to Monterey, and La Tulita is like a little wildcat ever since. She box my ears this morning when I tell her that the Americans are bandoleros, and say she never marry a Californian. And never Don Ramon Garcia, ay, yi!"

By this time the fine linen was floating at will upon the water, or lying in great heaps at the bottom of the clear pools. The suffering child scampered up through the pines with whoops of delight. The washing-women were pressed close about Faquita, who stood with thumbs on her broad hips, the fingers contracting and snapping as she spoke, wisps of hair bobbing back and forth about her shrewd black eyes and scolding mouth.

"Who is he? Where she meet him?" cried the audience. "Oh, thou old carreta! Why canst thou not talk faster?"

"If thou hast not more respect, Señorita Mariquita, thou wilt hear nothing. But it is this. There is a ball last night at Doña Maria Ampudia's house for La Tulita. She look hand- some, that witch! Holy Mary! When she walk it was like the tule in the river. You know. Why she have that name? She wear white, of course, but that frock—it is like the cobweb,

the cloud. She has not the braids like the other girls, but the
hair, soft like black feathers, fall down to the feet. And the
eyes like blue stars! You know the eyes of La Tulita. The
lashes so long, and black like the hair. And the sparkle! No
eyes ever sparkle like those. The eyes of Ysabel Herrera look
like they want the world and never can get it. Benicia's,
pobrecita, just dance like the child's. But La Tulita's! They
sparkle like the devil sit behind and strike fire out red-hot
iron—"

"Mother of God!" cried Mariquita, impatiently, "we all
know thou art daft about that witch! And we know how she
looks. Tell us the story."

"Hush thy voice or thou wilt hear nothing. It is this way. La
Tulita have the castanets and just float up and down the sala,
while all stand back and no breathe only when they shout. I
am in the garden in the middle the house, and I stand on a
box and look through the doors. Ay, the roses and the nastur-
tiums smell so sweet in that little garden! Well! She dance so
beautiful, I think the roof go to jump off so she can float up
and live on one the gold stars all by herself. Her little feet just
twinkle! Well! The door open and Lieutenant Ord come in.
He have with him another young man, not so handsome, but
so straight, so sharp eye and tight mouth. He look at La Tulita
like he think she belong to America and is for him. Lieutenant Ord go up to Doña Maria and say, so polite: 'I take the
liberty to bring Lieutenant'—I no can remember that name,
so American! 'He come today from San Diego and will stay
with us for a while.' And Doña Maria, she smile and say, very
sweet, 'Very glad when I have met all of our conquerors.' And
he turn red and speak very bad Spanish and look, look, at La
Tulita. Then Lieutenant Ord speak to him in English and he
nod the head, and Lieutenant Ord tell Doña Maria that his
friend like be introduced to La Tulita, and she say, 'Very
well,' and take him over to her who is now sit down. He ask
her to waltz right away, and he waltz very well, and then
they dance again, and once more. And then they sit down
and talk, talk. God of my soul, but the caballeros are mad!

And Doña Maria! By and by she can stand it no more and she
go up to La Tulita and take away from the American and say,
'Do you forget—and for a bandolero—that you are engage to
my nephew?' And La Tulita toss the head and say: 'How can I
remember Ramon Garcia when he is in Yerba Buena? I forget he is alive.' And Doña Maria is very angry. The eyes snap.
But just then the little sister of La Tulita run into the sala, the
face red like the American flag. 'Ay, Herminia!' she just gasp.
'The donas! The donas! It has come!' "

"The donas!" cried the washing-women, old and young.
"Didst thou see it, Faquita? Oh, surely. Tell us, what did he
send? Is he a generous bridegroom? Were there jewels? And
satins? Of what was the rosary?"

"Hush the voice or you will hear nothing. The girls all jump
and clap their hands and they cry: 'Come, Herminia. Come
quick! Let us go and see.' Only La Tulita hold the head very
high and look like the donas is nothing to her, and the Lieutenant look very surprise, and she talk to him very fast like
she no want him to know what they mean. But the girls just
take her hands and pull her out the house. I am after. La
Tulita look very mad, but she cannot help, and in five minutes we are at the Casa Rivera, and the girls scream and clap
the hands in the sala for Doña Carmen she have unpack the
donas and the beautiful things are on the tables and the sofas
and the chairs. Mother of God!"

"Go on! Go on!" cried a dozen exasperated voices.

"Well! Such a donas. Ay, he is a generous lover. A yellow
crêpe shawl embroidered with red roses. A white one with
embroidery so thick it can stand up. A string of pearls from
Baja California. (Ay, poor Ysabel Herrera!) Hoops of gold for
the little ears of La Tulita. A big chain of California gold. A set
of topaz with pearls all round. A rosary of amethyst—purple
like the violets. A big pin painted with the Ascension, and
diamonds all round. Silks and satins for gowns. A white lace
mantilla, Dios de mi alma! A black one for the visits. And the
nightgowns like cobwebs. The petticoats!" She stopped
abruptly.

"And the smocks?" cried her listeners, excitedly. "The smocks? They are more beautiful than Blandina's? They were pack in rose leaves—"

"Ay! yi! yi! yi!" The old woman dropped her head on her breast and waved her arms. She was a study for despair. Even she did not suspect how thoroughly she was enjoying herself.

"What! What! Tell us! Quick, thou old snail. They were not fine? They had not embroidery?"

"Hush the voices. I tell you when I am ready. The girls are like crazy. They look like they go to eat the things. Only La Tulita sit on the chair in the door with her back to all and look at the windows of Doña Maria. They look like a long row of suns, those windows.

"I am the one. Suddenly I say: 'Where are the smocks?' And they all cry: 'Yes, where are the smocks? Let us see if he will be a good husband. Doña Carmen, where are the smocks?'

"Doña Carmen turn over everything in a hurry. 'I did not think of the smocks,' she say. 'But they must be here. Everything was unpack in this room.' She lift all up, piece by piece. The girls help and so do I. La Tulita sit still but begin to look more interested. We search everywhere—everywhere—for twenty minutes. There—are—no—smocks!"

"God of my life! The smocks! He did not forget!"

"He forget the smocks!"

There was an impressive pause. The women were too dumfounded to comment. Never in the history of Monterey had such a thing happened before.

Faquita continued: "The girls sit down on the floor and cry. Doña Carmen turn very white and go in the other room. Then La Tulita jump up and walk across the room. The lashes fall down over the eyes that look like she is California and have conquer America, not the other way. The nostrils just jump. She laugh, laugh, laugh. 'So!' she say, 'my rich and generous and ardent bridegroom, he forget the smocks of the doñas. He proclaim as if by a poster on the streets that he will be a bad husband, a thoughtless, careless, indifferent husband. He has vow by the stars that he adore me. He has serenade beneath my window until I have beg for mercy. He persecute my mother. And now he flings the insult of insults in my teeth. And he with six married sisters!'

"The girls just sob. They can say nothing. No woman forgive that. Then she say loud, 'Ana,' and the girl run in. 'Ana,' she say, 'pack this stuff and tell José and Marcos take it up to the house of the Señor Don Ramon Garcia. I have no use for it.' Then she say to me: 'Faquita, walk back to Doña Maria's with me, no? I have engagement with the American.' And I go with her, of course; I think I go jump in the bay if she tell me; and she dance all night with that American. He no look at another girl—all have the eyes so red, anyhow. And Doña Maria is crazy that her nephew do such a thing, and La Tulita no go to marry him now. Ay, that witch! She have the excuse and she take it."

For a few moments the din was so great that the crows in a neighboring grove of willows sped away in fear. The women talked all at once, at the top of their voices and with no falling inflections. So rich an assortment of expletives, secular and religious, such individuality yet sympathy of comment, had not been called upon for duty since the seventh of July, a year before, when Commodore Sloat had run up the American flag on the Custom House. Finally they paused to recover breath. Mariquita's young lungs being the first to refill, she demanded of Faquita:—

"And Don Ramon—when does he return?"

"In two weeks, no sooner."

PART II

Two weeks later they were again gathered about the tubs.

For a time after arrival they forgot La Tulita—now the absorbing topic of Monterey—in a new sensation. Mariquita had appeared with a basket of unmistakable American underwear.

"What!" cried Faquita, shrilly. "Thou wilt defile these tubs with the linen of bandoleros? Hast thou had thy silly head turned with a kiss? Not one shirt shall go in this water."

Mariquita tossed her head defiantly. "Captain Brotherton say the Indian women break his clothes in pieces. They know not how to wash anything but dishrags. And does he not go to marry our Doña Eustaquia?"

"The Captain is not so bad," admitted Faquita. The indignation of the others also visibly diminished: the Captain had been very kind the year before when gloom lay heavy on the town. "But," continued the autocrat, with an ominous pressing of her lips, "sure he must change three times a day. Is all that Captain Brotherton's?"

"He wear many shirts," began Mariquita, when Faquita pounced upon the basket and shook its contents to the grass.

"Aha! It seems that the Captain has sometimes the short legs and sometimes the long. Sometimes he put the tucks in his arms, I suppose. What meaning has this? Thou monster of hypocrisy!"

The old women scowled and snorted. The girls looked sympathetic: more than one midshipman had found favor in the lower quarter.

"Well," said Mariquita, sullenly, "if thou must know, it is the linen of the Lieutenant of La Tulita. Ana ask me to wash it, and I say I will."

At this announcement Faquita squared her elbows and looked at Mariquita with snapping eyes.

"Oho, señorita, I suppose thou wilt say next that thou knowest what means this flirtation! Has La Tulita lost her heart, perhaps? And Don Ramon—dost thou know why he leaves Monterey one hour after he comes?" Her tone was sarcastic, but in it was a note of apprehension.

Mariquita tossed her head, and all pressed close about the rivals.

"What dost thou know, this time?" inquired the girl, provokingly. "Hast thou any letter to read today? Thou dost forget, old Faquita, that Ana is my friend—"

"Throw the clothes in the tubs," cried Faquita, furiously.

"Do we come here to idle and gossip? Mariquita, thou hussy, go over to that tub by thyself and wash the impertinent American rags. Quick. No more talk. The sun goes high."

No one dared to disobey the queen of the tubs, and in a moment the women were kneeling in irregular rows, tumbling their linen into the water, the brown faces and bright attire making a picture in the colorous landscape which some native artist would have done well to preserve. For a time no sound was heard but the distant roar of the surf, the sighing of the wind through the pines on the hill, the less romantic grunts of the women and the swish of the linen in the water. Suddenly Mariquita, the proscribed, exclaimed from her segregated tub:—

"Look! Look!"

Heads flew up or twisted on their necks. A party of young people, attended by a dueña, was crossing the meadow to the road. At the head of the procession were a girl and a man, to whom every gaze which should have been intent upon washing-tubs alone was directed. The girl wore a pink gown and a reboso. Her extraordinary grace made her look taller than she was; the slender figure swayed with every step. Her pink lips were parted, her blue starlike eyes looked upward into the keen cold eyes of a young man wearing the uniform of a lieutenant of the United States Army.

The dominant characteristics of the young man's face, even then, were ambition and determination, and perhaps the remarkable future was foreshadowed in the restless scheming mind. But today his deep-set eyes were glowing with a light more peculiar to youth, and whenever bulging stones afforded excuse he grasped the girl's hand and held it as long as he dared. The procession wound past the tubs and crossing the road climbed up the hill to the little wooded cemetery of the early fathers, the cemetery where so many of those bright heads were to lie forgotten beneath the wild oats and thistles.

"They go to the grave of Benicia Ortega and her little

one," said Francesca. "Holy Mary! La Tulita never look in a man's eyes like that before."

"But she have in his," said Mariquita, wisely.

"No more talk!" cried Faquita, and once more silence came to her own. But fate was stronger than Faquita. An hour later a little girl came running down, calling to the old woman that her grandchild, the consolation of her age, had been taken ill. After she had hurried away the women fairly leaped over one another in their efforts to reach Mariquita's tub.

"Tell us, tell us, chiquita," they cried, fearful lest Faquita's snubbing should have turned her sulky, "what dost thou know?"

But Mariquita, who had been biting her lips to keep back her story, opened them and spoke fluently.

"Ay, my friends! Doña Eustaquia and Benicia Ortega are not the only ones to wed Americans. Listen! La Tulita is mad for this man, who is no more handsome than the palm of my hand when it has all day been in the water. Yesterday morning came Don Ramon. I am in the back garden of the Casa Rivera with Ana, and La Tulita is in the front garden sitting under the wall. I can look through the doors of the sala and see and hear all. Such a handsome caballero, my friends! The gold six inches deep on the serape. Silver eagles on the sombrero. And the botas! Stamp with birds and leaves, ay, yi! He fling open the gates so bold, and when he see La Tulita he look like the sun is behind his face. (Such curls, my friends, tied with a blue ribbon!) But listen!

" 'Mi querida!' he cry, 'mi alma!' (Ay, my heart jump in my throat like he speak to me.) Then he fall on one knee and try to kiss her hand. But she throw herself back like she hate him. Her eyes are like the bay in winter. And then she laugh. When she do that, he stand up and say with the voice that shake:—

" 'What is the matter, Herminia? Do you not love me any longer?'

" 'I never love you,' she say. 'They give me no peace until I say I marry you, and as I love no one else—I do not care much. But now that you have insult me, I have the best excuse to break the engagement, and I do it.'

" 'I insult you?' He hardly can speak, my friends, he is so surprised and unhappy.

" 'Yes; did you not forget the smocks?'

" 'The—smocks!' he stammer, like that. 'The smocks?'

" 'No one can be blame but you,' she say. 'And you know that no bride forgive that. You know all that it means.'

" 'Herminia!' he say. 'Surely you will not put me away for a little thing like that!'

" 'I have no more to say,' she reply, and then she get up and go in the house and shut the door so I cannot see how he feel, but I am very sorry for him if he did forget the smocks. Well! That evening I help Ana water the flowers in the front garden, and every once in the while we look through the windows at La Tulita and the Lieutenant. They talk, talk, talk. He look so earnest and she—she look so beautiful. Not like a devil, as when she talk to Don Ramon in the morning, but like an angel. Sure, a woman can be both! It depends upon the man. By and by Ana go away, but I stay there, for I like look at them. After a while they get up and come out. It is dark in the garden, the walls so high, and the trees throw the shadows, so they cannot see me. They walk up and down, and by and by the Lieutenant take out his knife and cut a shoot from the rose-bush that climb up the house.

" 'These Castilian roses,' he say, very soft, but in very bad Spanish, 'they are very beautiful and a part of Monterey—a part of you. Look, I am going to plant this here, and long before it grow to be a big bush I come back and you will wear its buds in your hair when we are married in that lovely old church. Now help me,' and then they kneel down and he stick it in the ground, and all their fingers push the earth around it. Then she give a little sob and say, 'You must go?'

"He lift her up and put his arms around her tight. 'I must go,' he say. 'I am not my own master, you know, and the orders have come. But my heart is here, in this old garden, and I come back for it.' And then she put her arms around

him and he kiss her, and she love him so I forget to be sorry
for Don Ramon. After all, it is the woman who should be
happy. He hold her a long time, so long I am afraid Doña
Carmen come out to look for her. I lift up on my knees (I am
sit down before) and look in the window and I see she is
asleep, and I am glad. Well! After a while they walk up and
down again, and he tell her all about his home far away, and
about some money he go to get when the law get ready, and
how he cannot marry on his pay. Then he say how he go to be
a great general someday and how she will be the more beautiful woman in—how you call it?—Washington, I think. And
she cry and say she does not care, she only want him. And he
tell her water the rosebush every day and think of him, and
he will come back before it is large, and every time a bud
come out she can know he is thinking of her very hard."

"Ay, pobrecita!" said Francesca, "I wonder will he come
back. These men!"

"Surely. Are not all men mad for La Tulita?"

"Yes—yes, but he go far away. To America! Dios de mi
alma! And men, they forget." Francesca heaved a deep sigh.
Her youth was far behind her, but she remembered many
things.

"He return," said Mariquita, the young and romantic.

"When does he go?"

Mariquita pointed to the bay. A schooner rode at anchor.
"He go to Yerba Buena on that tomorrow morning. From
there to the land of the American. Ay, yi! Poor La Tulita! But
his linen is dry. I must take it to iron for I have it promised for
six in the morning." And she hastily gathered the articles
from the low bushes and hurried away.

That evening as the women returned to town, talking
gaily, despite the great baskets on their heads, they passed
the hut of Faquita and paused at the window to inquire for
the child. The little one lay gasping on the bed. Faquita sat
beside her with bowed head. An aged crone brewed herbs
over a stove. The dingy little house faced the hills and was

dimly lighted by the fading rays of the sun struggling through the dark pine woods.

"Holy Mary, Faquita!" said Francesca, in a loud whisper. "Does Liseta die?"

Faquita sprang to her feet. Her cross old face was drawn with misery. "Go, go!" she said, waving her arms, "I want none of you."

The next evening she sat in the same position, her eyes fixed upon the shrinking features of the child. The crone had gone. She heard the door open, and turned with a scowl. But it was La Tulita that entered and came rapidly to the head of the bed. The girl's eyes were swollen, her dress and hair disordered.

"I have come to you because you are in trouble," she said. "I, too, am in trouble. Ay, my Faquita!"

The old woman put up her arms and drew the girl down to her lap. She had never touched her idol before, but sorrow levels even social barriers.

"Pobrecita!" she said, and the girl cried softly on her shoulder.

"Will he come back, Faquita?"

"Surely, niñita. No man could forget you."

"But it is so far."

"Think of what Don Vicente do for Doña Ysabel, mi jita."

"But he is an American. Oh, no, it is not that I doubt him. He loves me! It is so far, like another world. And the ocean is so big and cruel."

"We ask the priest to say a mass."

"Ah, my Faquita! I will go to the church tomorrow morning. How glad I am that I came to thee." She kissed the old woman warmly, and for the moment Faquita forgot her trouble.

But the child threw out its arms and moaned. La Tulita pushed the hair out of her eyes and brought the medicine from the stove, where it simmered unsavorily. The child swallowed it painfully, and Faquita shook her head in despair. At the dawn it died. As La Tulita laid her white fingers on the gaping eyelids, Faquita rose to her feet. Her ugly old face was transfigured. Even the grief had gone out of it. For a moment she was no longer a woman, but one of the most subtle creations of the Catholic religion conjoined with racial superstitions.

"As the moon dieth and cometh to life again," she repeated with a sort of chanting cadence, "so man, though he die, will live again. Is it not better that she will wander forever through forests where crystal streams roll over golden sands, than grow into wickedness, and go out into the dark unrepenting, perhaps, to be bitten by serpents and scorched by lightning and plunged down cataracts?" She turned to La Tulita. "Will you stay here, señorita, while I go to bid them make merry?"

The girl nodded, and the woman went out. La Tulita watched the proud head and erect carriage for a moment, then bound up the fallen jaw of the little corpse, crossed its hands and placed weights on the eyelids. She pushed the few pieces of furniture against the wall, striving to forget the one trouble that had come into her triumphant young life. But there was little to do, and after a time she knelt by the window and looked up at the dark forest, upon which long shafts of light were striking, routing the fog that crouched in the hollows. The town was as quiet as a necropolis. The white houses, under the black shadows of the hills, lay like tombs. Suddenly the roar of the surf came to her ears, and she threw out her arms with a cry, dropping her head upon them and sobbing convulsively. She heard the ponderous waves of the Pacific lashing the keel of a ship.

She was aroused by shouting and sounds of merriment. She raised her head dully, but remembered in a moment what Faquita had left her to await. The dawn lay rosily on the town. The shimmering light in the pine woods was crossed and recrossed by the glare of rockets. Down the street came the sound of singing voices, the words of the song heralding the flight of a child-spirit to a better world. La Tulita slipped out of the back door and went to her home without meeting the procession. But before she shut herself in her room she awakened Ana, and giving her a purse of gold, bade her buy a little coffin draped with white and garlanded with white flowers.

PART III

"Tell us, tell us, Mariquita, does she water the rose tree every night?"

"Every night, ay, yi!"

"And is it big yet? Ay, but that wall is high! Not a twig can I see!"

"Yes, it grows!"

"And he comes not?"

"He write. I see the letters."

"But what does he say?"

"How can I know?"

"And she goes to the balls and meriendas no more. Surely, they will forget her. It is more than a year now. Someone else will be La Favorita."

"She does not care."

"Hush the voices," cried Faquita, scrubbing diligently. "It is well that she stay at home and does not dance away her beauty before he come. She is like a lily."

"But lilies turn brown, old Faquita, when the wind blow on them too long. Dost thou think he will return?"

"Surely," said Faquita, stoutly. "Could anyone forget that angel?"

"Ay, these men, these men!" said Francesca, with a sigh.

"Oh, thou old raven!" cried Mariquita. "But truly—truly— she has had no letter for three months."

"Aha, señorita, thou didst not tell us that just now."

"Nor did I intend to. The words just fell from my teeth."

"He is ill," cried Faquita, angrily. "Ay, my pobrecita! Sometimes I think Ysabel is more happy under the rocks."

"How dost thou know he is ill? Will he die?" The wash-tub

mail had made too few mistakes in its history to admit of doubt being cast upon the assertion of one of its officials.

"I hear Captain Brotherton read from a letter to Doña Eustaquia. Ay, they are happy!"

"When?"

"Two hours ago."

"Then we know before the town—like always."

"Surely. Do we not know all things first? Hist!"

The women dropped their heads and fumbled at the linen in the water. La Tulita was approaching.

She came across the meadow with all her old swinging grace, the blue gown waving about her like the leaves of a California lily when the wind rustled the forest. But the reboso framed a face thin and pale, and the sparkle was gone from her eyes. She passed the tubs and greeted the old women pleasantly, walked a few steps up the hill, then turned as if in obedience to an afterthought, and sat down on a stone in the shade of a willow.

"It is cool here," she said.

"Yes, señorita." They were not deceived, but they dared not stare at her, with Faquita's scowl upon them.

"What news has the wash-tub mail today?" asked the girl, with an attempt at lightness. "Did an enemy invade the South this morning, and have you heard it already, as when General Kearny came? Is General Castro still in Baja California, or has he fled to Mexico? Has Doña Prudencia Iturbi y Moncada given a ball this week at Santa Barbara? Have Don Diego and Doña Chonita—?"

"The young Lieutenant is ill," blurted out one of the old women, then cowered until she almost fell into her tub. Faquita sprang forward and caught the girl in her arms.

"Thou old fool!" she cried furiously. "Thou devil! Mayst thou find a tarantula in thy bed tonight. Mayst thou dream thou art roasting in hell." She carried La Tulita rapidly across the meadow.

"Ah, I thought I should hear there," said the girl, with a laugh. "Thank heaven for the wash-tub mail."

Faquita nursed her through a long illness. She recovered both health and reason, and one day the old woman brought her word that the young Lieutenant was well again—and that his illness had been brief and slight.

THE LAST

"Ay, but the years go quick!" said Mariquita, as she flapped a piece of linen after taking it from the water. "I wonder do all towns sleep like this. Who can believe that once it is so gay? The balls! The grand caballeros! The serenades! The meriendas! No more! No more! Almost I forget the excitement when the Americanos coming. I no am young anymore. Ay, yi!"

"Poor Faquita, she just died of old age," said a woman who had been young with Mariquita, spreading an article of underwear on a bush. "Her life just drop out like her teeth. No one of the old women that taught us to wash is here now, Mariquita. We are the old ones now, and we teach the young, ay, yi!"

"Well, it is a comfort that the great grow old like the low people. High birth cannot keep the skin white and the body slim. Ay, look! Who can think she is so beautiful before?"

A woman was coming down the road from the town. A woman, whom passing years had browned, although leaving the fine strong features uncoarsened. She was dressed simply in black, and wore a small American bonnet. The figure had not lost the slimness of its youth, but the walk was stiff and precise. The carriage evinced a determined will.

"Ay, who can think that once she sway like the tule!" said Mariquita, with a sigh. "Well, when she come today I have some news. A letter, we used to call it, dost thou remember, Brigida? Who care for the wash-tub mail now? These Americanos never hear of it, and our people—triste de mi—have no more the interest in anything."

"Tell us thy news," cried many voices. The older women had never lost their interest in La Tulita. The younger ones had heard her story many times, and rarely passed the wall before her house without looking at the tall rosebush which had all the pride of a young tree.

"No, you can hear when she come. She will come today. Six months ago today she come. Ay, yi, to think she come once in six months all these years! And never until today has the wash-tub mail a letter for her."

"Very strange she did not forget a Gringo and marry with a caballero," said one of the girls, scornfully. "They say the caballeros were so beautiful, so magnificent. The Americans have all the money now, but she been rich for a little while."

"All women are not alike. Sometimes I think she is more happy with the memory." And Mariquita, who had a fat lazy husband and a swarm of brown children, sighed heavily. "She live happy in the old house and is not so poor. And always she have the rosebush. She smile, now, sometimes, when she water it."

"Well, it is many years," said the girl, philosophically. "Here she come."

La Tulita, or Doña Herminia, as she now was called, walked briskly across the meadow and sat down on the stone which had come to be called for her. She spoke to each in turn, but did not ask for news. She had ceased long since to do that. She still came because the habit held her, and because she liked the women.

"Ah, Mariquita," she said, "the linen is not as fine as when we were young. And thou art glad to get the shirts of the Americans now. My poor Faquita!"

"Coarse things," said Mariquita, disdainfully. Then a silence fell, so sudden and so suggestive that Doña Herminia felt it and turned instinctively to Mariquita.

"What is it?" she asked rapidly. "Is there news today? Of what?"

Mariquita's honest face was grave and important.

"There is news, señorita," she said.

"What is it?"

The washing-women had dropped back from the tubs and were listening intently.

"Ay!" The oracle drew a long breath. "There is war over there, you know, señorita," she said, making a vague gesture toward the Atlantic states.

"Yes, I know. Is it decided? Is the North or the South victorious? I am glad that the wash-tub mail has not—"

"It is not that, señorita."

"Then what?"

"The Lieutenant—he is a great general now."

"Ay!"

"He has won a great battle—And—they speak of his wife, señorita."

Doña Herminia closed her eyes for a moment. Then she opened them and glanced slowly about her. The blue bay, the solemn pines, the golden atmosphere, the cemetery on the hill, the women washing at the stone tubs—all was unchanged. Only the flimsy wooden houses of the Americans scattered among the adobes of the town and the aging faces of the women who had been young in her brief girlhood marked the lapse of years. There was a smile on her lips. Her monotonous life must have given her insanity or infinite peace, and peace had been her portion. In a few minutes she said good-by to the women and went home. She never went to the tubs again.

THE LAST ANTELOPE

MARY AUSTIN (1868–1934)

Born at the stroke of midnight on September 9, 1868, at Carlinville, Illinois, Mary Austin was a rebel, a feminist, a mystic, and considered by many to be the most intelligent woman in the United States. "The Last Antelope" is from her book *Lost Borders* (1909), and demonstrates her expertise at writing poetically about human beings and nature coming into harmony. For Austin, as this story makes clear, the land of the American Southwest was a character. She once wrote:

> If the desert were a woman, I know well what like she would be: deep-breasted, broad in the hips, tawny, with tawny hair, great masses of it lying smooth along her perfect curves, full lipped like a sphinx, but not heavy-lidded like one, eyes sane and steady as the polished jewel of her skies, such a countenance as should make men serve without desiring her, such a largeness to her mind as should make their sins of no account, passionate, but not necessitous, patient—and you could not move her, no, not if you had all the earth to give, so much as one tawny hair's-breadth beyond her own desires.

There were seven notches in the juniper by the Lone Tree Spring for the seven seasons that Little Pete had summered there, feeding his flocks in the hollow of the Ceriso. The first time of coming he had struck his ax into the trunk, meaning to make firewood, but thought better of it, and thereafter chipped it in sheer friendliness, as one claps an old acquaintance, for by the time the flock has worked up the treeless windy stretch from the Little Antelope to the Ceriso, even a lone juniper has a friendly look. And Little Pete was a friendly man, though shy of demeanor, so that with the best will in the world for wagging his tongue, he could scarcely pass the time of day with good countenance; the soul of a jolly companion with the front and bearing of one of his own sheep.

He loved his dogs as brothers; he was near akin to the wild things; he communed with the huddled hills, and held intercourse with the stars, saying things to them in his heart that his tongue stumbled over and refused. He knew his sheep by name, and had respect to signs and seasons; his lips moved softly as he walked, making no sound. Well—what would you? a man must have fellowship in some sort.

Whoso goes a-shepherding in the desert hills comes to be at one with his companions, growing brutish or converting them. Little Pete humanized his sheep. He perceived lovable qualities in them, and differentiated the natures and dispositions of inanimate things.

Not much of this presented itself on slight acquaintance, for, in fact, he looked to be of rather less account than his own dogs. He was undersized and hairy, and had a roving eye; probably he washed once a year at the shearing as the sheep were washed. About his body he wore a twist of sheepskin with the wool outward, holding in place the tatters of his clothing. On hot days when he wreathed leaves about his head, and wove him a pent of twigs among the scrub in the middle of his flock, he looked a faun or some wood creature come out of pagan times, though no pagan, as was clearly shown by the medal of the Sacred Heart that hung on his hairy chest, worn open to all weathers. Where he went about sheep camps and shearings there were sly laughter and tapping of foreheads, but those who kept the tale of his flocks spoke well of him and increased his wage.

Little Pete kept to the same round year by year, breaking away from La Liebre after the spring shearing, south around the foot of Piños, swinging out to the desert in the wake of the quick, strong rains, thence to Little Antelope in July to drink a bottle for *Le Quatorze,* and so to the Ceriso by the time the poppy fires were burned quite out and the quail trooped at noon about the tepid pools. The Ceriso is not properly mesa nor valley, but a long-healed crater miles wide, rimmed about with the jagged edge of the old cone.

It rises steeply from the tilted mesa, overlooked by Black Mountain, darkly red as the red cattle that graze among the honey-colored hills. These are blunt and rounded, tumbling all down from the great crater and the mesa edge toward the long, dim valley of Little Antelope. Its outward slope is confused with the outlines of the hills, tumuli of blind cones, and the old lava flow that breaks away from it by the west gap and the ravine of the spring; within, its walls are deeply guttered by the torrent of winter rains.

In its cup-like hollow, the sink of its waters, salt and bitter as all pools without an outlet, waxes and wanes within a wide margin of bleaching reeds. Nothing taller shows in all the Ceriso, and the wind among them fills all the hollow with an eerie whispering. One spring rills down by the gorge of an old flow on the side toward Little Antelope, and, but for the lone juniper that stood by it, there is never a tree until you come to the foot of Black Mountain.

The flock of Little Pete, a maverick strayed from some rodeo, a prospector going up to Black Mountain, and a solitary antelope were all that passed through the Ceriso at any time. The antelope had the best right. He came as of old habit; he had come when the lightfoot herds ranged from here to the sweet, mist-watered cañons of the Coast Range, and the bucks went up to the windy mesas what time the young ran with their mothers, nose to flank. They had ceased before the keen edge of slaughter that defines the frontier of men.

All that a tardy law had saved to the district of Little Antelope was the buck that came up the ravine of the Lone Tree Spring at the set time of the year when Little Pete fed his flock in the Ceriso, and Pete averred that they were glad to see each other. True enough, they were each the friendliest thing the other found there; for though the law ran as far as the antelope ranged, there were hill-dwellers who took no account of it—namely, the coyotes. They hunted the buck in season and out, bayed him down from the feeding grounds, fended him from the pool, pursued him by relay races, ambushed him in the pitfalls of the black rock.

There were seven coyotes ranging the east side of the Ceriso at the time when Little Pete first struck his ax into the juniper tree, slinking, sly-footed, and evil-eyed. Many an evening the shepherd watched them running lightly in the hollow of the crater, the flash-flash of the antelope's white rump signaling the progress of the chase. But always the buck outran or outwitted them, taking to the high, broken ridges where no split foot could follow his seven-leagued bounds. Many a morning Little Pete, tending his cooking pot by a quavering sagebrush fire, saw the antelope feeding down toward the Lone Tree Spring, and looked his sentiments. The coyotes had spoken theirs all in the night with derisive voices; never was there any love lost between a shepherd and a coyote. The pronghorn's chief recommendation to an acquaintance was that he could outdo them.

After the third summer, Pete began to perceive a reciprocal friendliness in the antelope. Early mornings the shepherd saw him rising from his lair, or came often upon the warm pressed hollow where he had lain within cry of his coyote-scaring fire. When it was midday in the misty hollow and the shadows drawn close, stuck tight under the juniper and the sage, they went each to his nooning in his own fashion, but in the half light they drew near together.

Since the beginning of the law the antelope had half forgotten his fear of man. He looked upon the shepherd with steadfastness, he smelled the smell of his garments which was the smell of sheep and the unhandled earth, and the smell of wood smoke was in his hair. They had companionship without speech; they conferred favors silently after the manner of those who understand one another. The antelope led to the best feeding grounds, and Pete kept the sheep from muddying the spring until the buck had drunk. When the coyotes skulked in the scrub by night to deride him, the shepherd mocked them in their own tongue, and promised them the best of his lambs for the killing; but to hear afar off their hunting howl stirred him out of sleep to curse with great heartiness. At such times he thought of the antelope and wished him well.

Beginning with the west gap opposite the Lone Tree Spring about the first of August, Pete would feed all around the broken rim of the crater, up the gullies and down, and clean through the hollow of it in a matter of two months, or if the winter had been a wet one, a little longer, and in seven years the man and the antelope grew to know each other very well. Where the flock fed the buck fed, keeping farthest from the dogs, and at last he came to lie down with it.

That was after a season of scant rains, when the feed was poor and the antelope's flank grew thin; the rabbits had trooped down to the irrigated lands, and the coyotes, made more keen by hunger, pressed him hard. One of those smoky, yawning days when the sky hugged the earth, and all sound fell back from a woolly atmosphere and broke dully in the scrub, about the usual hour of their running between twilight and mid-afternoon, the coyotes drove the tall buck, winded, desperate, and foredone, to refuge among the silly sheep, where for fear of the dogs and the man the howlers dared not come. He stood at bay there, fronting the shepherd, brought up against a crisis greatly needing the help of speech.

Well—he had nearly as much gift in that matter as Little Pete. Those two silent ones understood each other; some assurance, the warrant of a free-given faith, passed between them. The buck lowered his head and eased the sharp throbbing of his ribs; the dogs drew in the scattered flocks; they moved, keeping a little cleared space nearest the buck; he moved with them; he began to feed. Thereafter the heart of Little Pete warmed humanly toward the antelope, and the coyotes began to be very personal in their abuse. That same night they drew off the shepherd's dogs by a ruse and stole two of his lambs.

The same seasons that made the friendliness of the antelope and Little Pete wore the face of the shepherd into a keener likeness to the weathered hills, and the juniper flourishing greenly by the spring bade fair to outlast them both. The line of plowed lands stretched out mile by mile from the lower valley, and a solitary homesteader built him a cabin at the foot of the Ceriso.

In seven years a coyote may learn somewhat; those of the Ceriso learned the ways of Little Pete and the antelope. Trust them to have noted, as the years moved, that the buck's flanks were lean and his step less free. Put it that the antelope was old, and that he made truce with the shepherd to hide the failing of his powers; then if he came earlier or stayed later than the flock, it would go hard with him. But as if he knew their mind in the matter, the antelope delayed his coming until the salt pool shrunk to its innermost ring of reeds, and the sun-cured grasses crisped along the slope. It seemed the brute sense waked between him and the man to make each aware of the other's nearness. Often as Little Pete drove in by the west gap he would sight the prongs of the buck rising over the barrier of black rocks at the head of the ravine. Together they passed out of the crater, keeping fellowship as far as the frontier of evergreen oaks. Here Little Pete turned in by the cattle fences to come at La Liebre from the north, and the antelope, avoiding all man-trails, growing daily more remote, passed into the wooded hills on unguessed errands of his own.

Twice the homesteader saw the antelope go up to the Ceriso at that set time of the year. The third summer when he sighted him, a whitish speck moving steadily against the fawn-colored background of the hills, the homesteader took down his rifle and made haste into the crater. At that time his cabin stood on the remotest edge of settlement, and the grip of the law was loosened in so long a reach.

"In the end the coyotes will get him. Better that he fall to me," said the homesteader. But, in fact, he was prompted by the love of mastery, which for the most part moves men into new lands, whose creatures they conceive given over into their hands.

The coyote that kept the watch at the head of the ravine saw him come, and lifted up his voice in the long-drawn dolorous whine that warned the other watchers in their unseen stations in the scrub. The homesteader heard also, and let a curse softly under his breath, for besides that they might scare his quarry, he coveted the howler's ears, in which the law upheld him. Never a tip nor a tail of one showed above the sage when he had come up into the Ceriso.

The afternoon wore on; the homesteader hid in the reeds, and the coyotes had forgotten him. Away to the left in a windless blur of dust the sheep of Little Pete trailed up toward the crater's rim. The leader, watching by the spring, caught a jackrabbit and was eating it quietly behind the black rock.

In the meantime the last antelope came lightly and securely by the gully, by the black rock and the lone juniper, into the Ceriso. The friendliness of the antelope for Little Pete betrayed him. He came with some sense of home, expecting the flock and protection of man-presence. He strayed witlessly into the open, his ears set to catch the jangle of the bells. What he heard was the snick of the breech-bolt as the homesteader threw up the sight of his rifle, and a small demoniac cry that ran from gutter to gutter of the crater rim, impossible to gauge for numbers or distance.

At that moment Little Pete worried the flock up the outward slope where the ruin of the old lava flows gave sharply back the wrangle of the bells. Three weeks he had won up from the Little Antelope, and three by way of the Sand Flat, where there was great scarcity of water, and in all that time none of his kind had hailed him. His heart warmed toward the juniper tree and the antelope whose hoofprints he found in the white dust of the mesa trail. Men had small respect by

Little Pete, women he had no time for: the antelope was the noblest thing he had ever loved. The sheep poured through the gap and spread fanwise down the gully; behind them Little Pete twirled his staff, and made merry wordless noises in his throat in anticipation of friendliness. "Ehu!" he cried when he heard the hunting howl, "but they are at their tricks again," and then in English he voiced a volley of broken, inconsequential oaths, for he saw what the howlers were about.

One imputes a sixth sense to that son of a thief misnamed the coyote, to make up for speech—persuasion, concerted movement—in short, the human faculty. How else do they manage the terrible relay races by which they make quarry of the fleetest-footed? It was so they plotted the antelope's last running in the Ceriso: two to start the chase from the black rock toward the red scar of a winter torrent, two to leave the mouth of the wash when the first were winded, one to fend the ravine that led up to the broken ridges, one to start out of the scrub at the base of a smooth upward sweep, and, running parallel to it, keep the buck well into the open; all these when their first spurt was done to cross leisurely to new stations to take up another turn. Round they went in the hollow of the crater, velvet-footed and sly even in full chase, and biding their time. It was a good running, but it was almost done when away by the west gap the buck heard the voice of Little Pete raised in adjuration and the friendly blether of the sheep. Thin spirals of dust flared upward from the moving flocks and signaled truce to chase. He broke for it with wide panting bounds and many a missed step picked up with incredible eagerness, the thin rim of his nostrils oozing blood. The coyotes saw and closed in about him, chopping quick and hard. Sharp ears and sharp muzzles cast up at his throat, and were whelmed in a press of gray flanks. One yelped, one went limping from a kick, and one went past him, returning with a spring upon the heaving shoulder, and the man in the reeds beside the bitter water rose up and fired.

All the luck of that day's hunting went to the homesteader,
for he had killed an antelope and a coyote with one shot, and
though he had a bad quarter of an hour with a wild and
loathly shepherd, who he feared might denounce him to the
law, in the end he made off with the last antelope, swung
limp and graceless across his shoulder. The coyotes came
back to the killing ground when they had watched him safely
down the ravine, and were consoled with what they found.
As they pulled the body of the dead leader about before they
began upon it, they noticed that the homesteader had taken
the ears of that also.

Little Pete lay in the grass and wept simply; the tears made
pallid traces in the season's grime. He suffered the torture,
the question extraordinary of bereavement. If he had not
lingered so long in the meadow of Los Robles, if he had
moved faster on the Sand Flat trail—but, in fact, he had come
up against the inevitable. He had been breathed upon by
that spirit which goes before cities like an exhalation and
dries up the gossamer and the dew.

From that day the heart had gone out of the Ceriso. It was a
desolate hollow, reddish-hued and dim, with brackish waters,
and moreover the feed was poor. His eyes could not forget
their trick of roving the valley at all hours; he looked by the
rill of the spring for hoofprints that were not there.

Fronting the west gap there was a spot where he would not
feed, where the grass stood up stiff and black with what had
dried upon it. He kept the flocks to the ridgy slopes where
the limited horizon permitted one to believe the crater was
not quite empty. His heart shook in the night to hear the
long-drawn hunting howl, and shook again remembering
that he had nothing to be fearing for. After three weeks he
passed out on the other side and came that way no more. The
juniper tree stood greenly by the spring until the homesteader cut it down for firewood. Nothing taller than the
rattling reeds stirs in all the hollow of the Ceriso.

WHEN THE COOK FELL ILL

B. M BOWER (1871-1940)

Born in Cleveland, Minnesota, Bertha Muzzy Bower moved to
Montana with her family at an early age. As Willa Cather, she
roamed the lands of her new home at every opportunity, familiariz-
ing herself with ranch life. "When the Cook Fell Ill," taken from her
collection of short stories *The Lonesome Trail* (1909), includes
among its characters members of the "Happy Family"—continuing
characters in her multivolume saga about the Flying U Ranch. In
this story, as in others, Bower portrays the settlers of the West—
whether ranchhands, doctors, or townfolk—not as lone, mythic heroes but rather as well-intentioned although sometimes incompe-
tent members of a family and/or community. "When the Cook Fell
Ill" also illustrates Bower's deft hand at creating comic situations
and characters.

It was four o'clock, and there was consternation in the
roundup camp of the Flying U; when one eats breakfast
before dawn—July dawn at that—covers thirty miles of
rough country before eleven o'clock dinner and as many
more after, supper seems, for the time being, the most important thing in the life of a cowboy.

Men stood about in various dejected attitudes, their
thumbs tucked inside their chap belts, blank helplessness
writ large upon their perturbed countenances—they were
the aliens, hired but to make a full crew during roundup.
Long-legged fellows with spurs a-jingle hurried in and out of
the cook tent, colliding often, shouting futile questions, com-

mands and maledictions—they were the Happy Family: loyal, first and last to the Flying U, feeling a certain degree of proprietorship and a good deal of responsibility.

Happy Jack was fanning an incipient blaze in the sheet-iron stove with his hat, his face red and gloomy at the prospect of having to satisfy fifteen outdoor appetites with his amateur attempts at cooking. Behind the stove, writhing bulkily upon a hastily unrolled bed, lay Patsy, groaning most pitiably.

"What the devil's the matter with that hot water?" Cal Emmett yelled at Happy Jack from the bedside, where he was kneeling sympathetically.

Happy Jack removed his somber gaze from the licking tongue of flame which showed in the stove front. "Fire ain't going good, yet," he said in a matter-of-fact tone which contrasted sharply with Cal's excitement. "Teakettle's dry, too. I sent a man to the crick for a bucket uh water; he'll be back in a minute."

"Well, *move!* If it was you tied in a knot with cramp, yuh wouldn't take it so serene."

"Aw, gwan. I got troubles enough, cooking chuck for this here layout. I got to have some help—and lots of it. Patsy ain't got enough stuff cooked up to feed a jackrabbit. Somebody's got to mosey in here and peel the spuds."

"That's your funeral," said Cal, unfeelingly.

Chip stuck his head under the lifted tent flap. "Say, I can't find that cussed Three-H bottle," he complained. "What went with it, Cal?"

"Ask Slim; he had it last. Ain't Shorty here, yet?" Cal turned again to Patsy, whose outcries were not nice to listen to. "Stay with it, old-timer; we'll have something hot to pour down yuh in a minute."

Patsy replied, but pain made him incoherent. Cal caught the word "poison," and then "corn"; the rest of the sentence was merely a succession of groans.

The face of Cal lengthened perceptibly. He got up and

went out to where the others were wrangling with Slim over the missing bottle of liniment.

"I guess the old boy's up against it good and plenty," he announced gravely. "He says he's poisoned; he says it was the corn."

"Well he had it coming to him," declared Jack Bates. "He's stuck that darned canned corn under our noses every meal since roundup started. He—"

"Oh, shut up," snarled Cal. "I guess it won't be so funny if he cashes in on the strength of it. I've known two or three fellows that was laid out cold with tin-can poison. It's sure fierce."

The Happy Family shifted uneasily before the impending tragedy, and their faces paled a little; for nearly every man of the range dreads ptomaine poisoning more than the bite of a rattler. One can kill a rattler, and one is always warned of its presence; but one never can tell what dire suffering may lurk beneath the gay labels of canned goods. But since one must eat, and since canned vegetables are far and away better than no vegetables at all, the Happy Family ate and took their chance—only they did not eat canned corn, and they had discussed the matter profanely and often with Patsy.

Patsy was a slave of precedent. Many seasons had he cooked beneath a roundup tent, and never had he stocked the mess wagon for a long trip and left canned corn off the list. It was good to his palate and it was easy to prepare, and no argument could wean him from imperturbably opening can after can, eating plentifully of it himself and throwing the rest to feed the gophers.

"Ain't there anything to give him?" asked Jack, relenting. "That Three-H would fix him up all right—"

"Dig it up, then," snapped Cal. "There's sure something got to be done, or we'll have a dead cook on our hands."

"Not even a drop uh whisky in camp!" mourned Weary. "Slim, you ought to be killed for getting away with that liniment."

Slim was too downhearted to resent the tone. "By golly, I

can't think what I done with it after I used it on Banjo. Seems like I stood it on that rock—"

"Oh, hell!" snorted Cal. "That's forty miles back."

"Say, it's sure a fright!" sympathized Jack Bates as a muffled shriek came through the cloth wall of the tent. "What's good for tincaneetis, I wonder?"

"A rattling good doctor," retorted Chip, throwing things recklessly about, still searching. "There goes the damn butter —pick it up, Cal."

"If Old Dock was sober, he could do something," suggested Weary. "I guess I'd better go after him; what do yuh think?"

"He could send out some stuff—if he was sober enough; he's sure wise on medicine."

Weary made him a cigarette. "Well, it's me for Dry Lake," he said, crisply. "I reckon Patsy can hang on till I get back; can poison doesn't do the business inside several hours, and he hasn't been sick long. He was all right when Happy Jack hit camp about two o'clock. I'll be back by dark—I'll ride Glory." He swung up on the nearest horse, which happened to be Chip's, and raced out to the saddle bunch a quarter of a mile away. The Happy Family watched him go and called after him, urging him unnecessarily to speed.

Weary did not waste time having the bunch corralled but rode in among the horses, his rope down and ready for business. Glory stared curiously, tossed his crimpled, silver mane, dodged a second too late and found himself caught.

It was unusual, this interruption just when he was busy cropping sweet grasses and taking his ease, but he supposed there was some good reason for it; at any rate he submitted quietly to being saddled and merely nipped Weary's shoulder once and struck out twice with an ivory-white, daintily rounded hoof—and Weary was grateful for the docile mood he showed.

He mounted hurriedly without a word of praise or condemnation, and his silence was to Glory more unusual than being roped and saddled on the range. He seemed to understand that the stress was great, and fairly bolted up the long, western slope of the creek bottom straight toward the slant of the sun.

For two miles he kept the pace unbroken, though the way was not of the smoothest and there was no trail to follow. Straight away to the west, with fifteen miles of hills and coulees between, lay Dry Lake; and in Dry Lake lived the one man in the country who might save Patsy.

"Old Dock" was a landmark among old-timers. The oldest pioneer found Dock before him among the Indians and buffalo that ran riot over the wind-brushed prairie where now the nation's beef feeds quietly. Why he was there no man could tell; he was a fresh-faced young Frenchman with much knowledge of medicine and many theories, and a reticence un-French. From the Indians he learned to use strange herbs that healed almost magically the ills of man; from the rough outcroppings of civilization he learned to swallow vile whiskey in great gulps, and to thirst always for more.

So he grew old while the West was yet young, until Dry Lake, which grew up around him, could not remember him as any but a white-bearded, stooped, shuffling old man who spoke a queer jargon and was always just getting drunk or sober. When he was sober his medicines never failed to cure; when he was drunk he could not be induced to prescribe, so that men trusted his wisdom at all times and tolerated his infirmities, and looked upon him with amused proprietorship.

When Weary galloped up the trail which, because a few habitations are strewn with fine contempt of regularity upon either side, is called by courtesy a street, his eyes sought impatiently for the familiar, patriarchal figure of Old Dock. He felt that minutes were worth much and that if he would save Patsy he must cut out all superfluities, so he resolutely declined to remember that cold, foamy beer refreshes one amazingly after a long, hot ride in the dust and the wind.

Upon the porch of Rusty Brown's place men were gathered, and it was evident even at a distance that they were mightily amused. Weary headed for the spot and stopped beside the hitching pole. Old Dock stood in the center of the group and his bent old figure was trembling with rage. With both hands he waved aloft his coat, on which was plastered a sheet of "tangle-foot" flypaper.

"Das wass de mean treeck!" he was shouting. "I don'd do de harm wis no mans. I tend mine business, I buy me mine clothes. De mans wass do dees treeck, he buy me new clothes —you bet you! Dass wass de mean—"

"Say, Dock," broke in Weary, towering over him, "you dig up some dope for tin-can poison, and do it quick. Patsy's took bad."

Old Dock looked up at him and shook his shaggy, white beard. "Das wass de mean treeck," he repeated, waving the coat at Weary. "You see dass? Mine coat, she ruint; dass was new coat!"

"All right—I'll take your word for it, Dock. Tell me what's good for tin—"

"Aw, I knows you fellers. You t'ink Ole Dock, she Dock, she don'd know nothings! You t'ink—"

Weary sighed and turned to the crowd. "Which end of a jag is this?" he wanted to know. "I've got to get some uh that dope-wisdom out uh him, somehow. Patsy's a goner, sure, if I don't connect with some medicine."

The men crowded close and asked questions which Weary felt bound to answer; everyone knew Patsy, who was almost as much a part of Dry Lake scenery as was Old Dock, and it was gratifying to a Flying U man to see the sympathy in their faces. But Patsy needed something more potent than sympathy, and the minutes were passing.

Old Dock still discoursed whimperingly upon the subject of his ruined coat and the meanness of mankind, and there was no weaning his interest for a moment, try as Weary would. And fifteen miles away in a picturesque creek bottom a man lay dying in great pain for want of one little part of the wisdom stored uselessly away in the brain of this drunken, doddering old man.

Weary's gloved hand dropped in despair from Old Dock's

bent shoulder. "Damn a drunkard!" he said bitterly, and got into the saddle. "Rusty, I'll want to borrow that calico cayuse uh yours. Have him saddled up right away, will yuh? I'll be back in a little bit."

He jerked his hat down to his eyebrows and struck Glory with the quirt; but the trail he took was strange to Glory and he felt impelled to stop and argue—as only Glory could argue —with his master. Minutes passed tumultuously, with nothing accomplished save some weird hoofprints in the sod. Eventually, however, Glory gave over trying to stand upon his head and his hind feet at one and the same instant, and permitted himself to be guided toward a certain tiny, low-eaved cabin in a meadow just over the hill from the town.

Weary was not by nature given to burglary, but he wrenched open the door of the cabin and went in, with not a whisper of conscience to say him nay. It was close and ill-smelling and very dirty inside, but after the first whiff Weary did not notice it. He went over and stopped before a little, old-fashioned chest; it was padlocked, so he left that as a last resort and searched elsewhere for what he wanted—medicine. Under the bed he found a flat, black case, such as old-fashioned doctors carried. He drew it out and examined it critically. This, also, was locked, but he shook it tentatively and heard the faintest possible jingle inside.

"Bottles," he said briefly, and grinned satisfaction. Something brushed against his hat and he looked up into a very dusty bunch of herbs. "You too," he told them, breaking the string with one yank. "For all I know, yuh might stand ace-high in this game. Lord! if I could trade brains with the old devil, just for tonight!"

He took a last look around, decided that he had found all he wanted, and went out and pulled the door shut. Then he tied the black medicine case to the saddle in a way that would give it the least jar, stuffed the bunch of dried herbs into his pocket and mounted for the homeward race. As he did so the sun threw a red beam into his eyes as though reminding him of the passing hours, and ducked behind the ridge which bounds Lonesome Prairie on the east.

The afterglow filled sky and earth with a soft, departing radiance when he stopped again in front of the saloon. Old Dock was still gesticulating wildly, and the sheet of flypaper still clung to the back of his coat. The crowd had thinned somewhat and displayed less interest; otherwise the situation had not changed, except that a pinto pony stood meekly, with head drooping, at the hitching pole.

"There's your horse," Rusty Brown called to Weary. "Yours played out?"

"Not on your life," Weary denied proudly. "When yuh see Glory played out, you'll see him with four feet in the air."

"I seen him that way half an hour ago, all right," bantered Bert Rogers.

Weary passed over the joke. "Mamma! Has it been that long?" he cried uneasily. "I've got to be moving some. Here, Dock, you put on that coat—and never mind the label; it's got to go—and so have you."

"Aw, he's no good to yuh, Weary," they protested. "He's too drunk to tell chloroform from dried apricots."

"That'll be all right," Weary assured them confidently. "I guess he'll be some sober by the time we hit camp. I went and dug up his dope-box, so he can get right to work when he arrives. Send him out here."

"Say, he can't never top off Powderface, Weary. I thought yuh was going to ride him yourself. It's plumb wicked to put that old centurion on him. He wouldn't be able to stay with him a mile."

"That's a heap farther than he could get with Glory," said Weary, unmoved. "Yuh don't seem to realize that Patsy's just next thing to a dead man, and Dock has got the name of what'll cure him sloshing around amongst all that whiskey in his head. I can't wait for him to sober up—I'm just plumb obliged to take him along, jag and all. Come on, Dock; this is a lovely evening for a ride."

Dock objected emphatically with head, arms, legs and

much mixed dialect. But Weary climbed down and, with the help of Bert Rogers, carried him bodily and lifted him into the saddle. When the pinto began to offer some objections, strong hands seized his bridle and held him angrily submissive.

"He'll tumble off, sure as yuh live," predicted Bert; but Weary never did things by halves; he shook his head and untied his coiled rope.

"By the Lord! I hate to see a man ride into town and pack off the only heirloom we got," complained Rusty Brown. "Dock's been handed down from generation to Genesis, and there ain't hardly a scratch on him. If yuh don't bring him back in good order, Weary Davidson, there'll be things doing."

Weary looked up from taking the last half-hitch around the saddle horn. "Yuh needn't worry," he said. "This medical monstrosity is more valuable to me than he is to you, right now. I'll handle him careful."

"Das wass de mean treeck!" cried Dock, for all the world like a parrot.

"It sure is, old boy," assented Weary cheerfully, and tied the pinto's bridle reins into a hard knot at the end. With the reins in his hand he mounted Glory. "Your pinto'll lead, won't he?" he asked Rusty then. It was like Weary to take a thing for granted first, and ask questions about it afterward.

"Maybe he will—he never did, so far," grinned Rusty. "It's plumb insulting to a self-respecting cow pony to make a packhorse out uh him. I wouldn't be none surprised if yuh heard his views on the subject before yuh git there."

"It's an honor to pack heirlooms," retorted Weary. "So long, boys."

Old Dock made a last, futile effort to free himself and then settled down in the saddle and eyed the world sullenly from under frost-white eyebrows heavy as a military mustache. He did not at that time look particularly patriarchal; more nearly he resembled a humbled, entrapped Santa Claus.

They started off quite tamely. The pinto leaned far back

upon the bridle reins and trotted with stiff, reluctant legs that did not promise speed; but still he went, and Weary drew a relieved breath. His arm was like to ache frightfully before they covered a quarter of the fifteen miles, but he did not mind that much; besides, he guessed shrewdly that the pinto would travel better once they were well out of town.

The soft, warm dusk of a July evening crept over the land and a few stars winked at them facetiously. Over by the reedy creek, frogs *cr-ek-ek-ekked* in a tuneless medley and nighthawks flapped silently through the still air, swooping suddenly with a queer, *whooing* rush like wind blowing through a cavern. Familiar sounds they were to Weary—so familiar that he scarce heard them; though he would have felt a vague, uneasy sense of something lost had they stilled unexpectedly. Out in the lane which led to the open range-land between wide reaches of rank blue-joint meadows, a new sound met them—the faint, insistent humming of mil-lions of mosquitoes. Weary dug Glory with his spurs and came near having his arm jerked from its socket before he could pull him in again. He swore a little and swung round in the saddle.

"Can't yuh dig a little speed into that cayuse with your heels, Dock?" he cried to the resentful heirloom. "We're going to be naturally chewed up if we don't fan the breeze along here."

"Ah don'd care—das wass de mean treeck!" growled Dock into his beard.

Weary opened his mouth, came near swallowing a dozen mosquitoes alive, and closed it again. What would it profit him to argue with a drunken man? He slowed till the pinto, still moving with stiff, reluctant knees, came alongside, and struck him sharply with his quirt; the pinto sidled and Dock lurched over as far as Weary's rope would permit.

"Come along, then!" admonished Weary, under his breath.

The pinto snorted and ran backward until Weary wished he had been content with the pace of a snail. Then the mos-quitoes swooped down upon them in a cloud and Glory struck out, fighting and kicking viciously. Presently Weary found himself with part of the pinto's bridle rein in his hand, and the memory of a pale object disappearing into the darkness ahead.

For the time being he was wholly occupied with his own horse; but when Glory was minded to go straight ahead instead of in a circle, he gave thought to his mission and thanked the Lord that Dock was headed in the right direction. He gave chase joyfully; for every mile covered in that fleet fashion meant an added chance for Patsy's life. Even the mosquitoes found themselves hopelessly out of the race and beat up harmlessly in the rear. So he galloped steadily upon the homeward trail; and a new discomfort forced itself upon his consciousness—the discomfort of swift riding while a sharp-cornered medicine-case of generous proportions thumped regularly against his leg. At first he did not mind it so much, but after ten minutes of riding so, the thing grew monotonously painful and disquieting to the nerves.

Five miles from the town he sighted the pinto; it was just disappearing up a coulee which led nowhere—much less to camp. Weary's self-congratulatory mood changed to impatience; he followed after. Two miles, and he reached the unclimbable head of the coulee—and no pinto. He pulled up and gazed incredulously at the blank, sandstone walls; searched long for some hidden pathway to the top and gave it up.

He rode back slowly under the stars, a much disheartened Weary. He thought of Patsy's agony and gritted his teeth at his own impotence. After a while he thought of Old Dock lashed to the pinto's saddle, and his conscience awoke and badgered him unmercifully for the thing he had done and the risk he had taken with one man's life that he might save the life of another.

Down near the mouth of the coulee he came upon a cattle trail winding up toward the stars. For the lack of a better clue he turned into it and urged Glory faster than was wise if he would save the strength of his horse; but Glory was game as long as he could stand, and took the hill at a lope with never a protest against the pace.

Up on the top the prairie stretched mysteriously away to the skyline, with no sound to mar the broody silence, and with never a movement to disturb the deep sleep of the grassland. All day had the hills been buffeted by a sweeping west wind; but the breeze had dropped with the sun, as though tired with roistering, and slept without so much as a dream-puff to shake the dew from the grasses.

Weary stopped to wind his horse and to listen, but not a hoofbeat came to guide him in his search. He leaned and shifted the medicine case a bit to ease his bruised leg, and wished he might unlock the healing mysteries and the magic stored within. It seemed to him a cruel world and unjust that knowledge must be gleaned slowly, laboriously, while men died miserably for want of it. Worse, that men who had gleaned should be permitted to smother such precious knowledge in the stupefying fumes of whiskey.

If he could only have appropriated Dock's brain along with his medicines, he might have been in camp by now, ministering to Patsy before it was too late to do anything. Without a doubt the boys were scanning anxiously the ridge, confident that he would not fail them though impatient for his coming. And here he sat helplessly upon a hilltop under the stars, many miles from camp, with much medicine just under his knee and a pocket crammed with an unknown, healing herb, as useless after all his effort as he had been in camp when they could not find the Three-H liniment.

Glory turned his head and regarded him gravely out of eyes near human in their questioning, and Weary laid caressing hand upon his silvery mane, grateful for the sense of companionship which it gave.

"You're sure a wise little nag," he said wistfully, and his voice sounded strange in the great silence. "Maybe you can find 'em—and if you can, I'll sure be grateful; you can paw the stars out uh high heaven and I won't take my quirt off my saddle horn; hope I may die if I do!"

Glory stamped one white hoof and pointed both ears straight forward, threw up his head and whinnied a shrill question into the night. Weary hopefully urged him with his knees. Glory challenged once again and struck out eagerly, galloping lightly in spite of the miles he had covered. Far back on the benchland came faint answer to his call, and Weary laughed from sheer relief. By the stars the night was yet young, and he grew hopeful—almost complacent.

Glory planted both forefeet deep in the prairie sod and skidded on the brink of a deep cut-bank. It was a close shave, such as comes often to those who ride the range by night. Weary looked down into blackness and then across into gloom. The place was too deep and sheer to ride into, and too wide to jump; clearly, they must go around it.

Going around a gully is not always the simple thing it sounds, especially when one is not sure as to the direction it takes. To find the head under such conditions requires time.

Weary thought he knew the place and turned north secure in the belief that the gully ran south into the coulee he had that evening fruitlessly explored. As a matter of fact it opened into a coulee north of them, and in that direction it grew always deeper and more impassable even by daylight.

On a dark night, with only the stars to guide one and to accentuate the darkness, such a discovery brings with it confusion of locality. Weary drew up when he could go no farther without plunging headlong into blackness, and mentally sketched a map of that particular portion of the globe and tried to find in it a place where the gulch might consistently lie. After a minute he gave over the attempt and admitted to himself that, according to his mental map, it could not consistently lie anywhere at all. Even Glory seemed to have lost interest in the quest and stood listlessly with his head down. His attitude irritated Weary very much.

"Yuh damn', taffy-colored cayuse!" he said fretfully. "This is as much your funeral as mine—seeing yuh started out all so brisk to find that pinto. Do yuh suppose yuh could find a horse if he was staked ten feet in front of your nose? Chances are, yuh couldn't. I reckon you'd have trouble finding your way around the little pasture at the ranch—unless the sun shone real bright and yuh had somebody to lead yuh!"

This was manifestly unjust and it was not like Weary; but this night's mission was getting on his nerves. He leaned and shifted the medicine case again, and felt ruefully of his bruised leg. That also was getting upon his nerves.

"Oh, Mamma!" he muttered disgustedly. "This is sure a sarcastic layout; dope enough here to cure all the sickness in Montana—if a fellow knew enough to use it—battering a hole in my leg you could throw a yearling calf into, and me wandering wild over the hills like a locoed sheepherder! Glory, you get a move on yuh, you knock-kneed, buzzard-headed—" He subsided into incoherent grumbling and rode back whence he came, up the gully's brim.

When the night was far gone and the slant of the Great Dipper told him that day-dawn was near, he heard a horse nicker wistfully, away to the right. Wheeling sharply, his spurs raking the roughened sides of Glory, he rode recklessly toward the sound, not daring to hope that it might be the pinto and yet holding his mind back from despair.

When he was near the place—so near that he could see a dim, formless shape outlined against the skyline—Glory stumbled over a sunken rock and fell heavily upon his knees. When he picked himself up he hobbled and Weary cursed him unpityingly.

When, limping painfully, Glory came up with the object, the heart of Weary rose up and stuck in his throat; for the object was a pinto horse and above it bulked the squat figure of an irate old man.

"Hello, Dock," greeted Weary. "How do yuh stack up?"

"*Mon Dieu*, Weary Davitson, I feex yous plandy. What for do you dees t'ing? I not do de harrm wis you. I not got de mooney wort' all dees troubles what you makes. Dees horse, she lak for keel me also. She buck, en keeck, en roon—*mon Dieu*, I not like dees t'ing."

"Sober, by thunder!" ejaculated Weary in an ecstatic half-whisper. "Dock, you've got a chance to make a record for yourself tonight—if we ain't too late," he added bodefully. "Do yuh know where we're headed for?"

"I t'ink for de devil," retorted Old Dock peevishly.

"No sir, we aren't. We're going straight to camp, and you're going to save old Patsy—you like Patsy, you know; many's the time you've tanked up together and then fell on each other's necks and wept because the good old times won't come again. He got poisoned on canned corn; the Lord send he ain't too dead for you to cure him. Come on—we better hit the breeze. We've lost a heap uh time."

"I not like dees rope; she not comforte. I have ride de bad horse when you wass in cradle."

Weary got down and went over to him. "All right, I'll unwind yuh. When we started, yuh know, yuh couldn't uh rode a rocking chair. I was plumb obliged to tie yuh on. Think we'll be in time to help Patsy? He was taken sick about four o'clock."

Old Dock waited till he was untied and the remnant of bridle rein was placed in his hand, before he answered ironically: "I not do de mageec, *mon cher* Weary. I mos' have de medicine or I can do nottings, I not wave de fingaire an' say de vord."

"That's all right—I've got the whole works. I broke into your shack and made a clean haul uh dope. And I want to tell yuh that for a doctor you've got blame poor ventilation to your house. But I found the medicine."

"Mon Dieu!" was the astonished comment, and after that they rode in silence and such haste as Glory's lameness would permit.

The first beams of the sun were touching redly the hilltops and the birds were singing from swaying weeds when they rode down the last slope into the valley where camped the Flying U.

The nighthawk had driven the horses into the rope-corral and men were inside watching, with spread loop, for a chance to throw. Happy Jack, with the cook's apron tied tightly around his lank middle, stood despondently in the doorway of the mess tent and said no word as they approached. In his silence—in his very presence there—Weary read disaster.

"I guess we're too late," he told Dock, in hushed tones; for the minute he hated the white-bearded old man whose drunkenness had cost the Flying U so dear. He slipped wearily from the saddle and let the reins drop to the ground. Happy Jack still eyed them silently.

"Well?" asked Weary, when his nerves would bear no more.

"When I git sick," said Happy Jack, his voice heavy with reproach, "I'll send *you* for help—if I want to die."

"Is he dead?" questioned Weary, in hopeless fashion.

"Well," said Happy Jack deliberately, "no, he ain't dead yet —but it's no thanks to *you*. Was it poker, or billiards? and who won?"

Weary looked at him dully a moment before he comprehended. He had not had any supper or any sleep, and he had ridden many miles in the long hours he had been away. He walked, with a pronounced limp on the leg which had been next the medicine case, to where Dock stood leaning shakily against the pinto.

"Maybe we're in time, after all," he said slowly. "Here's some kind uh dried stuff I got off the ceiling; I thought maybe yuh might need it—you're great on Indian weeds." He pulled a crumpled, faintly aromatic bundle of herbs from his pocket.

Dock took it and sniffed disgustedly, and dropped the herbs contemptuously to the ground. "Dat not wort' notting —she what you call—de—cat*neep.*" He smiled sourly.

Weary cast a furtive glance at Happy Jack, and hoped he had not overheard. Catnip! Still, how could he be expected to know what the blamed stuff was? He untied the black medicine case and brought it and put it at the feet of Old Dock. "Well, here's the joker, anyhow," he said. "It like to wore a hole clear through my leg, but I was careful and I don't believe any uh the bottles are busted."

Dock looked at it and sat heavily down upon a box. He looked at the case queerly, then lifted his shaggy head to gaze up at Weary. And behind the bleared gravity of his eyes was something very like a twinkle. "Dis, she not cure seek mans, neider. She—" He pressed a tiny spring which Weary had not discovered and laid the case open upon the ground. "You see?" he said plaintively. "She not good for Patsy—she tree dossen can-openaire."

Weary stared blankly. Happy Jack came up, looked and doubled convulsively. Can openers! Three dozen of them. Old Dock was explaining in his best English, and he was courteously refraining from the faintest smile.

"Dey de new, bettaire kind. I send for dem, I t'ink maybe I sell. I put her in de grip—so—I carry dem all togedder. My mediceen, she in de beeg ches'."

Weary had sat down and his head was dropped dejectedly into his hands. He had bungled the whole thing, after all. "Well," he said apathetically, "the chest was locked; I never opened it."

Old Dock nodded his head gravely. "She lock," he assented, gently. "She mooch mediceen—she wort' mooch mooney. De key, she in mine pocket—"

"Oh, I don't give a damn where the key is—now," flared Weary. "I guess Patsy'll have to cash in; that's all."

"Aw, gwan!" cried Happy Jack. "A sheepman come along just after you left, and he had a quart uh whiskey. We begged it off him and give Patsy a good bit jolt. That eased him up some, and we give him another—and he got to hollerin' so loud for more uh the same, so we just set the bottle in easy reach and let him alone. He's in there now, drunk as a biled owl—the lazy old devil. I had to get supper and breakfast too —and looks like I'd have to cook dinner. Poison—hell! I betche he never had nothing but a plain old bellyache!"

Weary got up and went to the mess tent, lifted the flap and looked in upon Patsy lying on the flat of his back, snoring

comfortably. He regarded him silently a moment, then
looked over his shoulder to where Old Dock huddled over
the three dozen can openers.

"Oh, Mamma!" he whispered, and poured himself a cup of
coffee.

THE VINE

MARI SANDOZ (1896–1966)

Born at Sandoz Post Office, Sheridan County, in northwestern Nebraska, Mari Sandoz endured many of the hardships of frontier life
that she would later incorporate into her stories. "The Vine," her
first published short story, was written in 1925 and appeared under
the pen name Marie Macumber in the January 1927 issue of the
newly founded magazine *Prairie Schooner*. The qualities she ad-
mired most in the works of her favorite writers, Joseph Conrad and
Thomas Hardy—"the overshadowing sense of fatality" and "the
inexorability of nature's laws"—are present in "The Vine." It is an
unusual story for the time it was written because of its tragic interpretation of the life of a pioneer woman.

The hill north of the little soddy rose tall and steep. Diagonal
cowpaths, grassing over, marked it into a regular pattern
from foot to sand-capped top. Soapweeds clustered about the
highest dune, catching the first late winter sun. Perhaps the
wind drove them over, like sheep, before the stinging sand,
Baldwin had said. Meda couldn't see anything in that. She
didn't see much in anything in Baldwin's world. She liked
green things, like the glory vine.

Meda couldn't see the narrow valley, wrinkled plush of
russet bunchgrass between the lower chophills with the wind
ruffling the pile as it fitfully passed. She saw the greedy thirst
of the long strip of gray that had been green corn in June. She
didn't hear the soughing of the wind across the valley. She

heard the crackle and snap of dry stems whipped by skeleton leaves.

Meda loved thick, green things like the glory vine that covered the window of the gray soddy and reached ambitiously toward the sod-covered eaves. The great heart-shaped leaves bobbed on their slender stems in the wind.

Tall and spare, she held her faded blue-checked apron back with one hand while she poured a dipper of water, brimming full, around the slender stalks, like tiny green pencils. The hungry sand soaked up the little pool, and as it vanished, Meda pushed dry sand over the wet spot from the edges with her broken shoe. She smoothed it over until it looked just as before—just as dry, just as yellow. Straightening up, she shaded her eyes and looked into the west, the northwest.

"There'll never be any rain," she told the vine. "I'll just have to water you." The thick leaves seemed to nod to her.

At the corners of the soddy, small holes, blowouts-to-be, spurted tiny volleys of sand as the wind playfully attacked the vine. Here and there a grain hit the window with a ping.

Standing in the whipping wind, Meda's body, in a long, faded, blue calico dress, looked hungry. Her hair, faded, straggled in the wind like raveled ends of old, weathered rope. Her hazel eyes looked hungry too, only too hungry to be fed. The smoldering yellow flame that lurked in their depths was hunger itself. Baldwin had told her to be careful of too much sunlight.

The glare outdoors blinded Meda as she stepped through the low doorway but she didn't need to see. She knew every detail of that crude room. She found the rocker near the window and swayed gently back and forth; her toes, bare and brown as saddle leather through the gaping holes in her shoes, dug little holes in the sand. The yellow flame died from her eyes, lost in the green shade of leaves that filtered the flecks of sunlight on the sand floor about her.

Meda looked about the room, its bareness old, old and yet strikingly new. Not even Baldwin could deny the smallness of the place, nor its shabbiness. An old grocery box covered with a frilled newspaper held the washbasin. The water pail stood beside the box on the sand. Newspaper frills, yellowed, lined the clock shelf, empty now. A flour-sack curtain, bleached on the grass to a blue-white, shut in the bed. A tablecloth of newer, creamier squares covered the two-legged table fastened to the wall. The kitchen corner was Baldwin's pride. It was a pickup, one pickup stove, pickup pipe and pickup frying pan. Only a few things, like the coffeepot and the saucepan, had been bought.

Two chairs, legs sunken into the sand, completed the furniture. "Not much to dust," Baldwin had said. What mattered dust, thought Meda, the yellow flaring up in her eyes. Even the walls would be dust if there were no roots to bind them into blocks. She sat still, her hands clenching and unclenching in her lap.

She compared it all to her Indiana home. She saw the cool porch, the shade trees. She wanted to see the rolling lawns of the chief citizen. She missed the small church bickerings and the news and gossip of the Ladies' Aid. Baldwin made light of the rivalry of neighbors over the parlor sets and crayon portraits. He despised the jealousies of the "folks back home." He even laughed at her charities "across the tracks," calling them inadequate, and he never could be dragged to a bazaar. Meda doted on these pastimes. She delighted in the slumming among what Baldwin termed "the unwashed." She felt she had lost her husband in this desert of soapweeds. He believed in the somnolent hills; he was a part of their simplicity, their strength. She thought resentfully of his frank enjoyment of their isolation.

Meda had felt nobly self-sacrificing when she came west with Baldwin. She had known they would soon go back home. But they hadn't, somehow, and now she hated it all. She hated the cold, she hated the heat. Blizzards, objects of wonder and delight to Baldwin, were days of disgust and loneliness to Meda. Not even the Indian summers nor the chinooks moved her. She cried for the cool green of the bluegrass meadows, never seeing the lovely, ever-changing browns and yellows of the hills.

A passionate fondness for green things grew on Meda. They made her think of Indiana. Crisp, green things, alien to the sun-yellowed hills. There had been a tall geranium that bore gorgeous red blossoms. A fall in the January mercury ended that. She had almost died; Baldwin had looked worried until spring brought the glory vine, with its deep red funnels against the slick, dark leaves. The red funnels died young; there was never any dew for them to catch, only heat, sun, and wind.

Meda had to admit she felt the hills, not like Baldwin, who felt a companionship in the purple hazes and the fiery evening sun. She feared the relentlessness of their long, lonesome days. But the nights were worse! Conversation was a skeleton of bones picked dry. She might look at the stars with Baldwin but they burned so far away. In the winter they were cold white lights mocking her from a blue steel sky. Meda hated them, as if they stood between her and the family circle where her brothers had always been frankly bored, but where her eyes hadn't burned, searing. . . .

Once, long ago, she had hated rain, too. It mussed the kitchen so, but now she would welcome it if any ever came. Then there was the cream and butter and fried chicken on Sundays or when the minister called. Meda remembered telling Baldwin that beans, always beans, palled so. He had replied, "They're a surefire crop."

Meda thought of dinner. She stepped out to squint at the sun. She saw windrows of dancing heat waves over the dunes south of the soddy. A tiny, puffball cloud of dust trailed its thin tail down the narrow strip of corn along the north slope. The crop looked even grayer than before. Nearer and nearer came the cloud until a team and then a man could be seen, the nucleus of the cloud. Baldwin walked, carefully jerking the handles of the corn plow to left and right. Meda knew the leaves of the small plants would rattle against the rusty wheels.

Back in the room, Meda lit the fire. Cowchips from the old candy pail (another pickup) and a handful of hay roared up the rusty pipe. The woman lifted a black kettle of beans from the oven. She poured a dipper of water over them. There would be soup again. Meda set the kettle on to boil. She never did like soup; she didn't like beans, either, but hunger would be appeased, even if it could demand only beans.

Baldwin could be heard outside. The snapping of the tugs in place across the horses' backs and the clatter of rings as the neckyoke dropped made Meda hurry. Baldwin came stooping through the doorway. His overalls were covered with dust. His blue eyes looked strangely light, like milky water, against his dirt-caked face. The long hair under his greasy Stetson was bleached to a taffy color with a frost of gray dust on it. Meda did not look up. She was busy poking chips into the cookstove. Her face was red with heat and her eyes reflected the leaping yellow flames as she broke the fuel into small pieces. There was a curl of distaste on her lip even though her hands were hidden with mammoth cotton gloves.

Baldwin poured out a scant cup of water. It rattled in the tin basin. He dipped his hands and rubbed his grimy face. Streaks of water ran down his neck in little rivulets. Pawing blindly along the wall, he grabbed the towel from its nail and rubbed it into his eyes. When he was through he ruefully surveyed the wreck. There wasn't a clean thread left. Meda, slipping off the gloves, saw the towel. She bit her lip, the yellow flames under her lashes danced. Baldwin held it out from him awkwardly.

"Never mind, Old Girl, I'll take them all to Twin Mills and wash them, next time I go."

Meda did not answer. She set the two bowls of soup upon the table and poured the coffee. Baldwin stood for a minute, looking at her, a little furrow between his brows. Then he set his large frame to the ridiculous table.

"Think that breeze will blow up something, Meda. I saw a swamp swallow skim the valley just before I came in." Baldwin salted his soup and broke little pieces of bread into the bowl.

Meda sat still, looking at the man. "I don't believe it can rain. It never does here. It's the going without water that is more than I can bear."

Baldwin looked up surprised. " 'Taint my fault it don't rain, or that the well went dry, is it? I'm no crazier than you about being just dampened 'stead of washed."

"It's not only the well." Meda's hands made a sweep of all the vast hills. "Three years of drouth, no corn, nothing but beans, beans. Is this what I left my home for? This—?"

She pushed her bowl back and, rising quickly, left the room. She stood outside, beside the window, her head touching the glory vine. The yellow flames in her eyes died sullenly down, like an ugly serpent before its charmer.

Baldwin ate steadily on. Meda heard the scraping of his spoon in the bottom of the dish and his cup being set down. After a few minutes she saw his pale blue eyes looking out between the leaves. They looked clouded, hurt. Well, she had been hurt too; just wait until he got numb. The flames flickered and flared up as Baldwin appeared at the door.

"Meda, you've said all that before but what can I do? Rain may come any day and fill the water hole, yes, and water that damned vine of yours."

Baldwin strode to the window and jerked away a leaf.

"Drouth don't seem to hurt it much. Probably gets my drinking water."

"No, no, I only give it dishwater, only dishwater." Meda shrank against the rooty sod beside the window. Her eyes gleamed orange.

"So? Only dishwater? And how much is that? Remember, I'm not skinning my horses, hauling water over seven miles of sand for you to drown dishes in."

Baldwin's lips had gone white. Meda watched as he viciously turned the corner of the shack. The yellow flames leaped and danced in her eyes. She flew to the corner in time to see Baldwin lift the heavy lids by their crosspieces from one barrel, then the other. He peered into the last and his jaw dropped. He slammed the lid down with a curse.

"Not even a gallon left and they ought to be half full."

Meda took a step backwards, then another. Not only had she lost her husband but he had turned enemy. Baldwin lifted the spade from its hook among the tools along the sod wall. Without looking at Meda he passed her and sank the blade deep into the soil at the roots of the vine. Meda's eyes grew round yellow flames, cold, hard. Her hands dropped limp as Baldwin stooped to snatch up a handful of the turned-up soil. He squeezed it and let it fall, a firm oval ball with deep finger creases.

"Soaked!" He looked at Meda. "Soaked, and I skimp myself and my horses while you . . ." Anger snapped in his pale opal eyes. He made one vengeful thrust at the base of the vine with the spade. Straightening up, he looked slowly at Meda. She was watching him, her hands covered, shielded in her apron. Baldwin walked stiffly to hang the spade in its place. Meda did not move or speak. Baldwin stood before her, expecting something, but she was puzzled. What could he expect? She had seen him angry before but usually he did something foolish before it melted.

Meda stood still as Baldwin led the horses to the wagon. With a rattle of rings and snap of teeth on bit the hitching up went on. Meda caught Baldwin looking at her over Old Bluche's back as he untied the lines. Circling the team around the soddy, Baldwin was out of sight. Two heavy thumps and he appeared from the north side with the two water barrels, blackened from sun and rain, in the wagon. Rusty hoops held down the flapping canvas squares that kept the lids on.

Baldwin kept looking back, over his shoulder, as he started down the valley. Standing up, feet wide apart, he flipped the lines and the team stepped up. His shout, "Be back before dark," came clearly above the bump-bump of the empty barrels as the wheels hit the bunchgrass. The wagon rattled across the valley and began its upward climb through the

sandy pass toward Twin Mills. Meda stood at the door, looking slowly all around the valley, her narrow horizon.

There was nothing to see. Heat waves danced over the
rolling chophills every day. Tiny whirlwinds often chased
each other across the narrow field. She didn't see the corn
blades, rising and dipping, merrily whirling upward and dipping again. They finally settled slowly into the tawny grass
and the fickle winds left them and hurried on to find other
playmates.

Meda turned from the heat and glare. Her eyes, resting on
the solid green thatch of the vine, became hazel again. She
held one of the leaves, cool even in the withering sun, between her hot palms. The larger leaves drooped a little; the
sun was too hot for them, thought Meda, as she pushed the
lump of soil Baldwin had lifted back into the hole with her
foot. Stepping on it easily, she tamped it back level with the
earth.

The sun drove her indoors and she cleared away the dinner dishes. There was no water to wash them, so she stacked
them in the empty black kettle and threw a dish towel over
them to keep out the flies. She wondered vaguely if there
would be a letter next freight day. She always wondered that,
but no one ever wrote anymore. Why should they? Mail once
a month discouraged correspondence easily with a piqued
family who didn't believe in Baldwin or in homesteading.

Then, too, there was seldom any respectable stationery,
and so the months slipped by and it was now a year since she
had written to anyone. There was nothing to say. The struggle to ignore the winter's blizzard or the summer's heat left
her with no news. She moved her hands, one over the other,
as she swayed in the rocker. The fire, yellow and fierce,
burned her eyeballs. She thought it was the sun, too. The
sand crunched softly under the rockers, falling from the
wood back into the trenches in fine streams.

The sun did not fleck the ground now. Crystal-clear blue
sky showed between the transparent leaves, like green
veined glass. Meda resented the blue. There was too much

blue, too much sky. If the whole sky could be green—that green of the leaves, seen from the inside of the room. Then she wouldn't have to look at the blue spots that made her eyes burn. She could look at the green. Somehow now she *had* to look at the sky; even closing her eyes didn't help much. She could see the blue over the rolling dunes that turned to blue and purple in the distance, turning all to blue where they met the sky. She tried to imagine her home, the apple orchard down the slope from the house, but the blues and purples and golden tans of the hills crept between, especially the blues.

Meda opened her eyes. There it was, blue, blue. Why, there was more blue than there had been, more than there was green, and the green looked brown, even gray!

Stumbling through the door, she ran to the vine and touched one of the leaves. It was limp. Another crumbled in her hands, almost powdery. She opened her palms and watched the wind blow the bits from them until all of the leaf was gone. The yellow flames leaped and danced in her unblinking eyes.

She flew into the house and carried the water pail to the plant. Upsetting it at the roots, Meda waited. Time would not go. The water seemed to stand, a little pool of blue sky. She crushed another leaf. The pool was still there, still blue. The leaves turned yellow, then gray. The pool was gone but the vine didn't grow fresh. The leaves began to rattle in the hot wind.

Meda stood very, very still. She wished the sky weren't so blue, it made her eyes burn. Suddenly she fell to her knees. She dug under the dry, crackling leaves, her hands clumsy with fear. She found it! The flame burned her; she buried her head in the leaves, the cut stalks in her palms. Her head dropped to her knees. The tendrils of the plant released the strings that held them and fell across her hair. Meda did not move.

A fan-shaped cloud hung in the northwest, gray and thin. It grew darker, slowly spreading its transparent fringe until the sun showed through, a white, round ball, without light. The cloud thickened, spread until the sun was gone. The rain began easily, a drop here and there. Then it stopped. The sand lay yellow with darker splotches, like freckles, but in a moment they were gone. Baldwin clucked up his team. They raised their heads and swung into a long stride that made the water barrels splash merrily. Baldwin looked at them and pulled the horses back to their slow walk. He sat sideways on the board used for a seat, turning his back to the rain that began again. Dusk stole down the gullies. The hills moved away in the darkness. The smell of wet horses came to his nostrils. He moved his foot and it struck a rusty syrup pail under the seat. He hoped Meda wouldn't mind too much when she saw what he had brought to replace the vine. He smiled into the darkness as he recalled how the greasy-looking woman at the cookhouse had gaped. Nesters weren't so popular at Twin Mills and here was one who wanted geranium slips! Well, he had them and a rooted wax plant "to boot."

Baldwin stripped the harness from the horses and turned them loose. He was soaked but he didn't mind. Water! and there might even be corn! He dug under the wagon seat for the syrup pail. As he lifted it he noticed that there was no light and there should have been a little, even through the vine and the rain. Perhaps Meda was asleep, he decided. Pail under arm, he went to the house. He felt for the knob, and didn't find anything, only a gap. Stepping nearer, he tried again. His hand struck the jamb. The door was open. He walked in and called softly, "Meda." No answer came and he called again, louder. His hands shook as he felt for a match. The first one sputtered, wet. The second match flared up and the darkness fell back. The wind whipped the flame and, shielding it with his cupped hand, he looked around the room. He took two steps to the bed and pulled back the white curtain. Both pillows sat up against the pine headboard, smooth and prim.

Baldwin lit the swinging bracket lamp and looked all about the room. The wick smoked; a black smudge grew up from one corner and spread over the globe to its fluted top. He stumbled over the pail of geranium slips in the doorway. He called "Meda" loudly, hands to his lips. There was a dim echo from the rain, nothing more.

Then he saw her crouched at the window. The vine had fallen all about her. The light came through the window clearly now, making little glittery streaks of the rain as it fell on the head of the woman.

He ran to her and lifted her in his arms, begging her to say what was the matter. She didn't answer, only whispered, always whispered. Baldwin set her into the rocker, trying to catch a word, but he couldn't. He pulled frantically at her knotted shoestring.

"Meda, are you sick? Meda, answer me."

She didn't notice him, but looked down at her hands full of the withered, soggy vine. Her lips moved and still Baldwin could not hear. He raised her face in his palm and his eyes went black with horror. In the lamplight her eyes roamed over his unknowingly, glowing like deep orange caves, alive with fierce, intense flames. She shrank down into the rocker like a frightened rabbit, clutching the vine to her breast.

"Who are you? You can't take my vine, my pretty green vine, you with the blue face."

Baldwin drew back, his hands clenched and white-knuckled. He tripped over the syrup pail with the rooted wax plant. It rolled away, spilling geranium slips over the sand.

MISTER DEATH AND THE REDHEADED WOMAN

HELEN EUSTIS (1916–)

Born in Cincinnati, Ohio, Helen Eustis attended Smith College, where she won a creative writing award. She has worked primarily as a translator but has written two novels. "Mister Death and the Redheaded Woman" appeared in the February 11, 1950, issue of *The Saturday Evening Post*. It is a rare example of a fantasy story set in the American West and memorable because of its unusual rhythmic style.

Mister Death come aridin' in from the plains on his pale stallion, ashootin' off his pistols, bangety-bang-bang, till you'd 'a thought some likkered-up Injun was on a spree. Hoo-ee! We was scared, all us little uns, and the grown folks, too, only to them he seemed more familiar.

But he never touched nary a soul that day but Billy-be-damn Bangtry, the one the girls was all crazy for. An' Mister Death no more'n just laid a finger on him, so he didn't die right off, but lay there cold and sweatin', dyin' of a bullet in his belly which was shot off by a drunken cowpoke in a wild euchre game.

Now, many a girl in our town wet the pillow with her tears when she heard how young Billy was like to die, for he was a handsome man and drove all women wild; but the one that cried and carried on the worst was pretty little Maude Applegate with the freckles and the red hair.

Old Injun Mary was anursin' Billy with poultices and healin' herbs, and wouldn't let no other woman near his door, so there wasn't nary a thing Maude Applegate could do for him. But you can't expect a redheaded woman to jest sit around and fret, like you would another color girl, an' Maude was no exception to that rule. Though she cried and carried on for a while, she pretty soon decided something had to be done, so she dried her eyes on her pettishirt, saddled up her daddy's pinto and took out across the plains after Mister Death.

Maude Applegate, she rode high and she rode low; she rode through the cow country into the sheep country; through the sheep country into the Injun country; through the Injun country to the far mountains, and there at last she caught up with Mister Death, jest about a mile down the trail from the little ole shack where he lived with his granny, up above the timberline.

When Maude Applegate spied his pale stallion, she was mighty tired and mighty weary; her red hair was all tumbled down her back, and her daddy's pinto wasn't no more'n skin and bone.

But she caught her breath and sang out loud, "Oh, wait up, Mister Death! Wait up for me!"

Mister Death, he pulled up his pale stallion and looked around surprised-like, for there isn't many that call out to halt him.

"Why, what you want, missy?" he asked Maude Applegate as she rode up alongside. "Jumpin' Jehoshaphat, if you don't look like you rode clean through the brier patch!"

"Oh, Mister Death," Maude panted out, "I rode high and I rode low after you! I rode through cow country into sheep country; through sheep country into Injun country; through Injun country to the far mountains, and all to ask you would you spare Billy-be-damn Bangtry, my own true love!"

At that, Mister Death throwed back his head so's his black sombrero slipped off and hung around his neck by the strings, and he laughed loud.

"Now ain't that cute!" said Mister Death. "Honey, I reckon you're jest about the cutest thing I'm likely to see!"

But Maude Applegate, she'd rode high and she'd rode low, she'd stood thirst and she'd stood hunger, she'd like to killed her daddy's pretty little pinto; futhermore, she was a redheaded woman, and she wasn't goin' to be laughed at so. She took and cussed out Mister Death good. She tole him that where she come from, no gentleman laughed at no lady in her true trouble, and she'd thank him to mind his manners with her, and she'd like to know who brought him up anyhow? Why, she knew dirty nekkid Injun bucks acted better'n him. She'd lay his mammy's aspinnin' in her grave, an' so on.

Well, Mister Death, he sobered down shortly and set up straight in his saddle and listened real still, with only his eyes ablinkin'. When Maude give out of breath, he took out his 'baccy bag, licked a paper an' rolled him a smoke.

"What'll you give me for Billy-be-damn Bangtry?" said he.

But Maude Applegate, she was really wound up. She tossed her red hair like a pony's mane and made a sassy mouth. "I ain't agonna talk business until I've washed my face and had me a bite to eat," said she. "I've rode high and I've rode low——"

"All right, all right!" said Mister Death. "Ride along now, and I'll take you to my cabin, where my ole granny'll take care of you."

So Maude and Mister Death they rode up the slope, Mister Death reinin' in his pale stallion to keep down to the pore tired pinto, until presently they come to a little ole shack with smoke comin' out of the stovepipe. There was Mister Death's granny astandin' in the door, as pleased as Punch to see some company.

"Why, you're right welcome, missy!" she sang out, soon's they were within callin' distance. "The pot's on the stove and the kettle's abilin'. Come right in and rest yourself a while!"

So they pulled up, and Mister Death swung down off his pale stallion, come around by Maude and lifted her right down to the ground, with his two big hands ameetin' around her little waist.

"Oh, ain't she the purty little thing?" his granny kept asayin' all the while, and hobblin' around the dooryard on her crutch like a bird with a broken wing. Then she taken Maude inside and give her warm water, and a ivory comb, and a pretty white silk wrapper from out of her ole brass-bound chest, and when Mister Death come in from seein' to the hosses, there's Maude Applegate asettin' like a redheaded angel, drinkin' tea.

Maude, she perked up soon's she got some vittles inside her, and presently she had Mister Death and his granny laughin' fit to bust with her comical tales of the folks back home.

Soon Mister Death, he set in to yawnin' and gapin'. "I've rode a far piece today," he said to his granny. "I been twice around the world and back, and I think I'll lay my head in your lap and catch forty winks." And shortly he was asnorin'.

Then Death's granny begun to talk low to Maude Applegate, questionin' her all about herself, and where she come from, and why she come. So Maude tole her all about how Billy-be-damn Bangtry, her own true love, lay adyin' of a bullet in his belly, so what could she do but take out after Mister Death to beg him to stay his hand? When Death's granny had heard the whole story she fetched a great sigh.

"Well," she said, "it's a great pity to me you got your heart set, for you're like the girl I once was, and if I had my way, you're the girl I'd choose for my grandson to marry, for I'm ole and tired and would like to see him settled before I go to my rest. You're young, and you're purty, and you don't stand for no sass, and if my ole eyes don't deceive me, you can do a bit of witchin' too. Now ain't that true?"

"Well," Maude answered her modestly, "jest a little of the plain."

"Like what now?" said Death's granny. "White or black?"

"Little o' both," said Maude. "Witched my little brother into passin' his arithmetic, and I also witched the preacher's wife so she tripped on her shoestring and fell in the horse trough."

Once more Death's granny fetched a sigh. "That's a good start for a young'un," said she. "Don't look to me like a girl like you ought to waste herself on no drunken gamblin' cowhand gets hisself shot up in some fool card game. Howsomever, if you got your heart set, I'll help you. Whenever Death catnaps this way, he shortly begins to talk in his sleep, and when he talks, he'll answer three questions truly, and then wake up. What shall I ask him for you?"

"Ask him," said Maude right away, "what is his price to let off Billy-be-damn Bangtry."

"That's one," said Death's granny. "You got three questions. What else?"

At this, Maude had to think, and presently she said, "Ask him why he took my baby sister from her cradle."

"Very well, chile," said Granny. "And one more."

Then Maude Applegate bent her red head near to the red fire and was still, but at last she said, kinda low and slow, "Ask him what he does when he's lonesome."

To this, Death's granny answered nothing at all, and so they set in quiet until shortly Death begun to mumble in his sleep. Then his granny took aholt of a lock of his coal-black hair and tweaked it, gentle-like.

"Yes?" Death said, but without wakin' up. "Yes?"

"Tell me, son," Death's granny said, bendin' over his ear. "What will you take to let off Billy-be-damn Bangtry?"

At this, Death twitched and turned in his sleep. "Oh, Granny," he said, "she's such a pretty girl! If it was some, I'd make it an eye. An' if it was others, I'd make it ten years o' life. But for her, I'll make it that she must ride with me two times around the world and give me a kiss on the lips."

At this, Maude drawed a great deep breath and leaned back in her chair.

"Well, son," said Granny, "here's another question she asks of you. Why did you take her baby sister from the cradle?"

Then Death twisted and turned in his sleep again. "She

was sick," he said. "She was full of pain. I took her so she need never cry no more."

At this, Maude bowed her head and hid her cheek in her hand.

"Well, son," said Death's granny, "an here's the last. What is it you do when you're lonesome?"

At this, Death give a regular heave and a great groan, and turned his face from the light of the fire. For a long time he whispered and mumbled, and finally he said real low, "I peep through the windows at how the human bein's sleep in each other's arms."

And with this last, he woke up with a jerk, give a mighty yawn, sayin', "My stars, I must of dropped off!"

Now Mister Death and his granny was cheerful folks in spite o' his profession, and that evenin' they gave Maude Applegate such a high ole time that she was almost glad she come. Death's granny, she tole some mighty edifyin' stories about her young days, and futhermore, she got out a jug of her blackberry wine, and Death, he played such merry tunes on his fiddle that Maude Applegate got right out of her chair, picked up her skirts and danced. It was late that night when Death's granny showed Maude to the little trundle bed all made up fresh beside her own four-poster.

In the mornin', Death's granny had Maude's own dress all mended and pressed for her, and a fine breakfast of coffee and ham and grits to stay their stomachs for their long trip, and when Mister Death brought round his pale stallion, all saddled and bridled to go, the tears was standin' in his granny's eyes as she kissed Maude Applegate good-by.

"Good-by," Maude said. "I thank you for your fine hospitality, and if it wasn't for Billy-be-damn Bangtry, my own true love, I'd be right sorry to go."

Mister Death, he lifted Maude up to his big stallion and leaped astride; then away they rode, right up the snowy mountaintop into the sky, and Maude Applegate was surprised to find herself warm and comfortable, ridin' pillion with her arms wrapped around Mister Death's waist.

Then didn't they have a ride! Mister Death, he rode his
pale stallion up the mountains of the storm to the pastures of
the sky, where the little clouds was grazin' beside their big
fat white mammies, and the big black daddy clouds kept
watch around the edge. And he rode up in the fields where
the stars grow, and let Maude Applegate pluck a few to wear
in her red hair. He rode past the moon, and when Maude
Applegate reached out and touched it, it was cold as snow,
and slippery too. They couldn't go too near the sun, Mister
Death said, lest they might get burned.

But Mister Death, he had his business to tend to, so pretty
soon they set out across the wide ocean on their way to twice
around the world. Mister Death, he wrapped Maude in his
cloak of invisibility, and he took her to all sorts of houses in all
sorts of climes—houses where Chinee folks lived, and
Rooshian, and Japanee, and African, and folks that never
spoke a word of English since the day they was born. He
showed her castles and dirty little huts the like of which she
never seen in all the state of Texas; he showed her kings and
princes and poor folks and all, and maybe she didn't just open
her eyes! But in one respect she noticed they was all alike:
when Mister Death come, the living couldn't see him, and
wept and wailed, but the folks that was dyin' rose up to greet
him, and smiled at him on their way, like they knew him for a
friend. She was right glad to see that everybody didn't take
him for such a bad fellow after all. While they rode, Mister
Death, he tole Maude Applegate many a pretty tale about his
far travels, and it was plain to see he was a man knew more'n
likker and women and ridin' herd.

And when they was on their last lap around and on their
way home, Mister Death, he rode out over the ocean and
showed Maude Applegate where the whales played—she
saw 'em just as plain, aplowin' through the clear green water
like a herd of buffalo on a grassy plain. And he rode over the
North Pole, for her to see the polar bears, which was all white
but for their noses, and he showed her the crocodiles of
Egypt driftin' down the Nile, and the tigers of India, too, and

every strange creature with his mate. And at last Maude Applegate couldn't help feeling sorry for Mister Death, that he was the only one who had to be alone in all the whole wide world.

But at last they was lopin' back over the plain toward our town; they seen the smoke arisin' from the stovepipes and chimleys into the pale blue sky; they rode right down the main street past Tarbell's Emporium, past the Wells Fargo office, and reined up before the Blue Bird Saloon.

"Why, what you pullin' up here for?" Maude Applegate asked of Mister Death, feelin' surprised, but Mister Death only answered, "Ne'mind; you'll see," and swung down out of the saddle.

Then he reached up and lifted Maude down from off his pale stallion, and he wrapped her once more in his cloak of invisibility, and he said to her, "Now fer the rest of the bargain."

So Maude stood there with her eyes shut, kinda stiff, and steelin' herself for his kiss, but nothin' happened at all, so she opened 'em again, and Mister Death said to her, "No, Maude, the bargain was that you was to kiss me."

So Maude, she was obliged to ask Mister Death to lean down his head, which he did, and she was obliged to reach up and put her mouth on his. Now maybe she thought it would be cold, and maybe she thought it would be fearful to kiss Mister Death—I don't know, I'm sure—but it surely come as a great surprise to her when she found her two arms around his neck without her knowin' how they got there, and her own two lips on his, and the truth of the matter is, it was Mister Death stepped away the first, and tole her, soft and low, "Run along now, Maude. Billy-be-damn Bangtry, your own true love, is settin' right in there in the Blue Bird Saloon."

Then Mister Death unwrapped her from his cloak of invisibility, so's she couldn't see him no more—only hear his spurs jinglin' as he walked away—and Maude Applegate was left standin' by herself before the Blue Bird Saloon, where, inside the window, she could see Billy-be-damn Bangtry, her own true love, settin' at a table drinkin' whiskey with a bunch of fly young women of a kind doesn't mind settin' in saloons. Oh, then Maude Applegate's bosom was so full of a thousand feelin's she thought she would bust, and she didn't know whether what she wanted most was to wrench up the hitchin' rail, bust into the Blue Bird Saloon and lambaste her own true love, or whether she'd simply like to melt of shame and sink through the ground. Then she noticed that her daddy's pinto, all groomed and saddled, was tied up by the Blue Bird door. She was jest about decided to mount him and gallop off home before anybody seen her, when Billy-be-damn Bangtry caught a sight of her through the window, and come pushin' out the swingin' doors, swaggerin' and hitchin' his pants like he'd never been half dead in his life.

"Why," he sings out, "if it ain't little Maude Applegate waitin' for me outside the Blue Bird Saloon! Where you been, honey? Heared you was away."

Maude Applegate, she felt the red comin' up in her face. She snapped back at him, "Heared you was mighty sick."

"Mighty sick," Billy said, shakin' his head. "Mighty sick and like to die, but ole Injun Mary, she doctored me good as new with her poultices and herbs!"

Now this was the last straw to Maude Applegate. She'd rode high and she'd rode low; she'd rode through cow country to sheep country; through sheep country to Injun country; through Injun country to the far mountains, all to stay the hand of Mister Death from taking Billy-be-damn Bangtry, her own true love; she'd rode twice around the world and back and give a kiss on the lips to a strange man, and all to save a feller which turned out to be this horse-smellin', whiskey-breathin', tobaccer-chewin', loose-livin', gamblin', no-good cow hand standin' here lookin' at her like she was a ripe peach an' all he had to do was shake the tree. Maude Applegate was so mad she could of cried, but she didn't do no such of a thing, since she was a redheaded woman, and besides, somethin' better come to her mind.

Just then she seen ole Pap Tarbell lean outen the upstairs winder of Tarbell's Emporium, and Maude, she took and witched a spell. When Pap let fly with his tobaccer juice, Maude, she witched it straight into Billy-be-damn Bangtry's eye. And while he was still standin' there acussin' and a-swearin' in such language as no lady cares to hear, Maude unhitched her daddy's little pinto pony and leaped astride. She dug in her heels and set the dust aflyin' as she galloped down the street out of town. She rode through cow country into sheep country, through sheep country into Injun country, through Injun country to the far mountains, until she caught sight of Mister Death on his pale stallion.

Then she sung out, "Oh, wait up, Mister Death! Wait up for me!"

And when Mister Death heard her he turned and rode back down the trail—though he is one who turns back for no man—and he snatched her off her little pinto and onto his pale stallion, he held her close and he kissed her good and pretty soon he said, "I guess Granny'll be mighty proud to see you."

And Maude Applegate said to him, "Jest don't let me hear no talk about peepin' through folks' windows never no more."

Now Maude Applegate she lived long and happy with Mister Death, and from all I hear, she's with him yet. Fact is, she took to helpin' him with his work, and when we was little uns, and cross at bedtime, and startin' to cry, our mammies'd tell us, "Hush, now, honey, close your eyes and pretty soon Maude Applegate'll sit by your bed and sing you a lullaby."

And she used to too. Heard her myself.

LOST SISTER

DOROTHY M. JOHNSON
(1905–)

Generally recognized as the First Lady of Western fiction, Dorothy
M. Johnson was born in McGregor, Iowa, and grew up in Montana.
"Lost Sister" was collected in *The Hanging Tree* (1957) and won the
Spur Award from the Western Writers of America for best short
story of 1956. It was later made into a chamber opera by James
Eversole entitled *Bessie*. The story is loosely based on the capture of
Cynthia Ann Parker by the Comanches. Aunt Bessie, the "lost sis-
ter" recaptured by the whites, seems to me one of the finest of
Johnson's many unforgettable female characters. Both Aunt Bessie
and Dorothy M. Johnson command our respect.

Our household was full of women, who overwhelmed my
Uncle Charlie and sometimes confused me with their bustle
and chatter. We were the only men on the place. I was nine
years old when still another woman came—Aunt Bessie, who
had been living with the Indians.

When my mother told me about her, I couldn't believe it.
The savages had killed my father, a cavalry lieutenant, two
years before. I hated Indians and looked forward to wiping
them out when I got older. (But when I was grown, they were
no menace anymore.)

"What did she live with the hostiles for?" I demanded.

"They captured her when she was a little girl," Ma said.
"She was three years younger than you are. Now she's coming home."

High time she came home, I thought. I said so, promising, "If they was ever to get me, I wouldn't stay with 'em long."

Ma put her arms around me. "Don't talk like that. They won't get you. They'll never get you."

I was my mother's only real tie with her husband's family. She was not happy with those masterful women, my Aunts Margaret, Hannah and Sabina, but she would not go back East where she came from. Uncle Charlie managed the store the aunts owned, but he wasn't really a member of the family —he was just Aunt Margaret's husband. The only man who had belonged was my father, the aunts' younger brother. And I belonged, and someday the store would be mine. My mother stayed to protect my heritage.

None of the three sisters, my aunts, had ever seen Aunt Bessie. She had been taken by the Indians before they were born. Aunt Mary had known her—Aunt Mary was two years older—but she lived a thousand miles away now and was not well.

There was no picture of the little girl who had become a legend. When the family had first settled here, there was enough struggle to feed and clothe the children without having pictures made of them.

Even after army officers had come to our house several times and there had been many letters about Aunt Bessie's delivery from the savages, it was a long time before she came. Major Harris, who made the final arrangements, warned my aunts that they would have problems, that Aunt Bessie might not be able to settle down easily into family life.

This was only a challenge to Aunt Margaret, who welcomed challenges. "She's our own flesh and blood," Aunt Margaret trumpeted. "Of course she must come to us. My poor, dear sister Bessie, torn from her home forty years ago!"

The major was earnest but not tactful. "She's been with the savages all those years," he insisted. "And she was only a little girl when she was taken. I haven't seen her myself, but it's reasonable to assume that she'll be like an Indian woman."

My stately Aunt Margaret arose to show that the audience

was ended. "Major Harris," she intoned, "I cannot permit anyone to criticize my own dear sister. She will live in my home, and if I do not receive official word that she is coming within a month, I shall take steps."

Aunt Bessie came before the month was up.

The aunts in residence made valiant preparations. They bustled and swept and mopped and polished. They moved me from my own room to my mother's—as she had been begging them to do because I was troubled with nightmares. They prepared my old room for Aunt Bessie with many small comforts—fresh doilies everywhere, hairpins, a matching pitcher and bowl, the best towels and two new nightgowns in case hers might be old. (The fact was that she didn't have any.)

"Perhaps we should have some dresses made," Hannah suggested. "We don't know what she'll have with her."

"We don't know what size she'll take, either," Margaret pointed out. "There'll be time enough for her to go to the store after she settles down and rests for a day or two. Then she can shop to her heart's content."

Ladies of the town came to call almost every afternoon while the preparations were going on. Margaret promised them that, as soon as Bessie had recovered sufficiently from her ordeal, they should all meet her at tea.

Margaret warned her anxious sisters, "Now, girls, we mustn't ask her too many questions at first. She must rest for a while. She's been through a terrible experience." Margaret's voice dropped way down with those last two words, as if only she could be expected to understand.

Indeed Bessie had been through a terrible experience, but it wasn't what the sisters thought. The experience from which she was suffering, when she arrived, was that she had been wrenched from her people, the Indians, and turned over to strangers. She had not been freed. She had been made a captive.

Aunt Bessie came with Major Harris and an interpreter, a half-blood with greasy black hair hanging down to his shoulders. His costume was half army and half primitive. Aunt Margaret swung the door open wide when she saw them coming. She ran out with her sisters following, while my mother and I watched from a window. Margaret's arms were outstretched, but when she saw the woman closer, her arms dropped and her glad cry died.

She did not cringe, my Aunt Bessie who had been an Indian for forty years, but she stopped walking and stood staring, helpless among her captors.

The sisters had described her often as a little girl. Not that they had ever seen her, but she was a legend, the captive child. Beautiful blond curls, they said she had, and big blue eyes—she was a fairy child, a pale-haired little angel who ran on dancing feet.

The Bessie who came back was an aging woman who plodded in moccasins, whose dark dress did not belong on her bulging body. Her brown hair hung just below her ears. It was growing out; when she was first taken from the Indians, her hair had been cut short to clean out the vermin.

Aunt Margaret recovered herself and, instead of embracing this silent stolid woman, satisfied herself by patting an arm and crying, "Poor dear Bessie, I am your sister Margaret. And here are our sisters Hannah and Sabina. We do hope you're not all tired out from your journey!"

Aunt Margaret was all graciousness, because she had been assured beyond doubt that this was truly a member of the family. She must have believed—Aunt Margaret could believe anything—that all Bessie needed was to have a nice nap and wash her face. Then she would be as talkative as any of them.

The other aunts were quick-moving and sharp of tongue. But this one moved as if her sorrows were a burden on her bowed shoulders, and when she spoke briefly in answer to the interpreter, you could not understand a word of it.

Aunt Margaret ignored these peculiarities. She took the party into the front parlor—even the interpreter, when she understood there was no avoiding it. She might have gone on battling with the major about him, but she was in a hurry to talk to her lost sister.

"You won't be able to converse with her unless the interpreter is present," Major Harris said. "Not," he explained hastily, "because of any regulation, but because she has forgotten English."

Aunt Margaret gave the half-blood interpreter a look of frowning doubt and let him enter. She coaxed Bessie. "Come, dear, sit down."

The interpreter mumbled, and my Indian aunt sat cautiously on a needlepoint chair. For most of her life she had been living with people who sat comfortably on the ground.

The visit in the parlor was brief. Bessie had had her instructions before she came. But Major Harris had a few warnings for the family. "Technically, your sister is still a prisoner," he explained, ignoring Margaret's start of horror. "She will be in your custody. She may walk in your fenced yard, but she must not leave it without official permission.

"Mrs. Raleigh, this may be a heavy burden for you all. But she has been told all this and has expressed willingness to conform to these restrictions. I don't think you will have any trouble keeping her here." Major Harris hesitated, remembered that he was a soldier and a brave man, and added, "If I did, I wouldn't have brought her."

There was the making of a sharp little battle, but Aunt Margaret chose to overlook the challenge. She could not overlook the fact that Bessie was not what she had expected.

Bessie certainly knew that this was her lost white family, but she didn't seem to care. She was infinitely sad, infinitely removed. She asked one question: "Mary?" and Aunt Margaret almost wept with joy.

"Sister Mary lives a long way from here," she explained, "and she isn't well, but she will come as soon as she's able. Dear sister Mary!"

The interpreter translated this, and Bessie had no more to say. That was the only understandable word she ever did say in our house, the remembered name of her older sister.

When the aunts, all chattering, took Bessie to her room, one of them asked, "But where are her things?"

Bessie had no things, no baggage. She had nothing at all but the clothes she stood in. While the sisters scurried to bring a comb and other oddments, she stood like a stooped monument, silent and watchful. This was her prison. Very well, she would endure it.

"Maybe tomorrow we can take her to the store and see what she would like," Aunt Hannah suggested.

"There's no hurry," Aunt Margaret declared thoughtfully. She was getting the idea that this sister was going to be a problem. But I don't think Aunt Margaret ever really stopped hoping that one day Bessie would cease to be different, that she would end her stubborn silence and begin to relate the events of her life among the savages, in the parlor over a cup of tea.

My Indian aunt accustomed herself, finally, to sitting on the chair in her room. She seldom came out, which was a relief to her sisters. She preferred to stand, hour after hour, looking out the window—which was open only about a foot, in spite of all Uncle Charlie's efforts to budge it higher. And she always wore moccasins. She was never able to wear shoes from the store, but seemed to treasure the shoes brought to her.

The aunts did not, of course, take her shopping after all. They made her a couple of dresses; and when they told her, with signs and voluble explanations, to change her dress, she did.

After I found that she was usually at the window, looking across the flat land to the blue mountains, I played in the yard so I could stare at her. She never smiled, as an aunt should, but she looked at me sometimes, thoughtfully, as if measuring my worth. By performing athletic feats, such as walking on my hands, I could get her attention. For some reason, I valued it.

She didn't often change expression, but twice I saw her scowl with disapproval. Once was when one of the aunts slapped me in a casual way. I had earned the slap, but the Indians did not punish children with blows. Aunt Bessie was shocked, I think, to see that white people did. The other time was when I talked back to someone with spoiled, small-boy insolence—and that time the scowl was for me.

The sisters and my mother took turns, as was their Christian duty, in visiting her for half an hour each day. Bessie didn't eat at the table with us—not after the first meal.

The first time my mother took her turn, it was under protest. "I'm afraid I'd start crying in front of her," she argued, but Aunt Margaret insisted.

I was lurking in the hall when Ma went in. Bessie said something, then said it again, peremptorily, until my mother guessed what she wanted. She called me and put her arm around me as I stood beside her chair. Aunt Bessie nodded, and that was all there was to it.

Afterward, my mother said, "She likes you. And so do I." She kissed me.

"I don't like her," I complained. "She's queer."

"She's a sad old lady," my mother explained. "She had a little boy once, you know."

"What happened to him?"

"He grew up and became a warrior. I suppose she was proud of him. Now the army has him in prison somewhere. He's half Indian. He was a dangerous man."

He was indeed a dangerous man, and a proud man, a chief, a bird of prey whose wings the army had clipped after bitter years of trying.

However, my mother and my Indian aunt had that one thing in common: they both had sons. The other aunts were childless.

There was a great to-do about having Aunt Bessie's photograph taken. The aunts who were stubbornly and valiantly trying to make her one of the family wanted a picture of her for the family album. The government wanted one too, for some reason—perhaps because someone realized that a

thing of historic importance had been accomplished by re-
covering the captive child.

Major Harris sent a young lieutenant with the greasy-
haired interpreter to discuss the matter in the parlor. (Margaret, with great foresight, put a clean towel on a chair and
saw to it the interpreter sat there.) Bessie spoke very little
during that meeting, and of course we understood only what
the half-blood *said* she was saying.

No, she did not want her picture made. No.

But your son had his picture made. Do you want to see it?
They teased her with that offer, and she nodded.

If we let you see his picture, then will you have yours
made?

She nodded doubtfully. Then she demanded more than
had been offered: If you let me keep his picture, then you can
make mine.

No, you can only look at it. We have to keep his picture. It
belongs to us.

My Indian aunt gambled for high stakes. She shrugged and
spoke, and the interpreter said, "She not want to look. She
will keep or nothing."

My mother shivered, understanding as the aunts could not
understand what Bessie was gambling—all or nothing.

Bessie won. Perhaps they had intended that she should.
She was allowed to keep the photograph that had been made
of her son. It has been in history books many times—the half-
white chief, the valiant leader who was not quite great
enough to keep his Indian people free.

His photograph was taken after he was captured, but you
would never guess it. His head is high, his eyes stare with
boldness but not with scorn, his long hair is arranged with
care—dark hair braided on one side and with a tendency to
curl where the other side hangs loose—and his hands hold
the pipe like a royal scepter.

That photograph of the captive but unconquered warrior
had its effect on me. Remembering him, I began to control
my temper and my tongue, to cultivate reserve as I grew

older, to stare with boldness but not scorn at people who annoyed or offended me. I never met him, but I took silent pride in him—Eagle Head, my Indian cousin.

Bessie kept his picture on her dresser when she was not holding it in her hands. And she went like a docile, silent child to the photograph studio, in a carriage with Aunt Margaret early one morning, when there would be few people on the street to stare.

Bessie's photograph is not proud but pitiful. She looks out with no expression. There is no emotion there, no challenge, only the face of an aging woman with short hair, only endurance and patience. The aunts put a copy in the family album.

But they were nearing the end of their tether. The Indian aunt was a solid ghost in the house. She did nothing because there was nothing for her to do. Her gnarled hands must have been skilled at squaws' work, at butchering meat and scraping and tanning hides, at making tepees and beading ceremonial clothes. But her skills were useless and unwanted in a civilized home. She did not even sew when my mother gave her cloth and needles and thread. She kept the sewing things beside her son's picture.

She ate (in her room) and slept (on the floor) and stood looking out the window. That was all, and it could not go on. But it had to go on, at least until my sick Aunt Mary was well enough to travel—Aunt Mary who was her older sister, the only one who had known her when they were children.

The sisters' duty visits to Aunt Bessie became less and less visits and more and more duty. They settled into a bearable routine. Margaret had taken upon herself the responsibility of trying to make Bessie talk. Make, I said, not teach. She firmly believed that her stubborn and unfortunate sister needed only encouragement from a strong-willed person. So Margaret talked, as to a child, when she bustled in:

"Now there you stand, just looking, dear. What in the world is there to see out there? The birds—are you watching the birds? Why don't you try sewing? Or you could go for a little walk in the yard. Don't you want to go out for a nice little walk?"

Bessie listened and blinked.

Margaret could have understood an Indian woman's not being able to converse in a civilized tongue, but her own sister was not an Indian. Bessie was white, therefore she should talk the language her sisters did—the language she had not heard since early childhood.

Hannah, the put-upon aunt, talked to Bessie too, but she was delighted not to get any answers and not to be interrupted. She bent over her embroidery when it was her turn to sit with Bessie and told her troubles in an unending flow. Bessie stood looking out the window the whole time.

Sabina, who had just as many troubles, most of them emanating from Margaret and Hannah, went in like a martyr, firmly clutching her Bible, and read aloud from it until her time was up. She took a small clock along so that she would not, because of annoyance, be tempted to cheat.

After several weeks Aunt Mary came, white and trembling and exhausted from her illness and the long, hard journey. The sisters tried to get the interpreter in but were not successful. (Aunt Margaret took that failure pretty hard.) They briefed Aunt Mary, after she had rested, so the shock of seeing Bessie, would not be too terrible. I saw them meet, those two.

Margaret went to the Indian woman's door and explained volubly who had come, a useless but brave attempt. Then she stood aside, and Aunt Mary was there, her lined white face aglow, her arms outstretched. "Bessie! Sister Bessie!" she cried.

And after one brief moment's hesitation, Bessie went into her arms and Mary kissed her sun-dark, weathered cheek. Bessie spoke. "Ma-ry," she said. "Ma-ry." She stood with tears running down her face and her mouth working. So much to tell, so much suffering and fear—and joy and triumph, too—and the sister there at last who might legitimately hear it all and understand.

But the only English word that Bessie remembered was "Mary," and she had not cared to learn any others. She turned to the dresser, took her son's picture in her work-hardened hands, reverently, and held it so her sister could see. Her eyes pleaded.

Mary looked on the calm, noble, savage face of her half-blood nephew and said the right thing: "My, isn't he handsome!" She put her head on one side and then the other. "A fine boy, sister," she approved. "You must"—she stopped, but she finished—"be awfully proud of him, dear!"

Bessie understood the tone if not the words. The tone was admiration. Her son was accepted by the sister who mattered. Bessie looked at the picture and nodded, murmuring. Then she put it back on the dresser.

Aunt Mary did not try to make Bessie talk. She sat with her every day for hours and Bessie did talk—but not in English. They sat holding hands for mutual comfort while the captive child, grown old and a grandmother, told what had happened in forty years. Aunt Mary said that was what Bessie was talking about. But she didn't understand a word of it and didn't need to.

"There is time enough for her to learn English again," Aunt Mary said. "I think she understands more than she lets on. I asked her if she'd like to come and live with me, and she nodded. We'll have the rest of our lives for her to learn English. But what she has been telling me—she can't wait to tell that. About her life, and her son."

"Are you sure, Mary dear, that you should take the responsibility of having her?" Margaret asked dutifully, no doubt shaking in her shoes for fear Mary would change her mind now that deliverance was in sight. "I do believe she'd be happier with you, though we've done all we could."

Margaret and the other sisters would certainly be happier with Bessie somewhere else. And so, it developed, would the United States government.

Major Harris came with the interpreter to discuss details, and they told Bessie she could go, if she wished, to live with

Mary a thousand miles away. Bessie was patient and willing, stolidly agreeable. She talked a great deal more to the interpreter than she had ever done before. He answered at length and then explained to the others that she wanted to know how she and Mary would travel to this far country. It was hard, he said, for her to understand just how far they were going.

Later we knew that the interpreter and Bessie had talked about much more than that.

Next morning, when Sabina took breakfast to Bessie's room, we heard a cry of dismay. Sabina stood holding the tray, repeating, "She's gone out the window! She's gone out the window!"

And so she had. The window that had always stuck so that it would not raise more than a foot was open wider now. And the photograph of Bessie's son was gone from the dresser. Nothing else was missing except Bessie and the decent dark dress she had worn the day before.

My Uncle Charlie got no breakfast that morning. With Margaret shrieking orders, he leaped on a horse and rode to the telegraph station.

Before Major Harris got there with half a dozen cavalrymen, civilian scouts were out searching for the missing woman. They were expert trackers. Their lives had depended, at various times, on their ability to read the meaning of a turned stone, a broken twig, a bruised leaf. They found that Bessie had gone south. They tracked her for ten miles. And then they lost the trail, for Bessie was as skilled as they were. Her life had sometimes depended on leaving no stone or twig or leaf marked by her passage. She traveled fast at first. Then, with time to be careful, she evaded the followers she knew would come.

The aunts were stricken with grief—at least Aunt Mary was—and bowed with humiliation about what Bessie had done. The blinds were drawn, and voices were low in the house. We had been pitied because of Bessie's tragic folly in having let the Indians make a savage of her. But now we were traitors because we had let her get away.

Aunt Mary kept saying pitifully, "Oh, why did she go? I thought she would be contented with me!"

The others said that it was, perhaps, all for the best.

Aunt Margaret proclaimed, "She has gone back to her own." That was what they honestly believed, and so did Major Harris.

My mother told me why she had gone. "You know that picture she had of the Indian chief, her son? He's escaped from the jail he was in. The fort got word of it, and they think Bessie may be going to where he's hiding. That's why they're trying so hard to find her. They think," my mother explained, "that she knew of his escape before they did. They think the interpreter told her when he was here. There was no other way she could have found out."

They scoured the mountains to the south for Eagle Head and Bessie. They never found her, and they did not get him until a year later, far to the north. They could not capture him that time. He died fighting.

After I grew up, I operated the family store, disliking storekeeping a little more every day. When I was free to sell it, I did, and went to raising cattle. And one day, riding in a canyon after strayed steers, I found—I think—Aunt Bessie. A cowboy who worked for me was along, or I would never have let anybody know.

We found weathered bones near a little spring. They had a mystery on them, those nameless human bones suddenly come upon. I could feel old death brushing my back.

"Some prospector," suggested my riding partner.

I thought so too until I found, protected by a log, sodden scraps of fabric that might have been a dark, respectable dress. And wrapped in them was a sodden something that might have once been a picture.

The man with me was young, but he had heard the story of the captive child. He had been telling me about it, in fact. In the passing years it had acquired some details that surprised me. Aunt Bessie had become once more a fair-haired beauty, in this legend that he had heard, but utterly sad and silent. Well, sad and silent she really was.

I tried to push the sodden scrap of fabric back under the log, but he was too quick for me. "That ain't no shirt, that's a dress!" he announced. "This here was no prospector—it was a woman!" He paused and then announced with awe, "I bet you it was your Indian aunt!"

I scowled and said, "Nonsense. It could be anybody."

He got all worked up about it. "If it was *my* aunt," he declared, "I'd bury her in the family plot."

"No," I said, and shook my head.

We left the bones there in the canyon, where they had been for forty-odd years if they were Aunt Bessie's. And I think they were. But I would not make her a captive again. She's in the family album. She doesn't need to be in the family plot.

If my guess about why she left us is wrong, nobody can prove it. She never intended to join her son in hiding. She went in the opposite direction to lure pursuit away.

What happened to her in the canyon doesn't concern me, or anyone. My Aunt Bessie accomplished what she set out to do. It was not her life that mattered, but his. She bought him another year.

GERANIUM HOUSE
PEGGY SIMSON CURRY (1911–)

Peggy Simson Curry was born in Dunure, Ayrshire, Scotland, and grew up in Colorado. She has received two Spur Awards from the Western Writers of America and in 1981 was named Poet Laureate of Wyoming, where she presently makes her home. "Geranium House" was first published in the anthology *Frontiers West* (1959). Set in Wyoming, it is a charming story about an indigent married couple who take up residence in an abandoned homesteader's shack. Curry effectively blends pathos and humor, and the story serves as an interesting contrast to Mari Sandoz's treatment of the pioneer experience in "The Vine."

We heard about them long before we saw them. News traveled fast in those days even though we didn't have telephones in the valley. Old Gus, the mailman, gave us the full report. "They come in from Laramie in a two-wheeled cart," he said, "him ridin' and her walkin' beside the cart and the old sway-bellied horse pullin' it. That cart was mostly filled with plants, and she was carrying one in her arms, just like most women carry a baby."

"Where they going to live?" my Uncle Rolfe asked.

"They moved into that old homestead shack on the flats," Gus said. "Been there since the Indians fired the west range, that shack. Used to belong to a man named Matt but he died a spell ago, and I guess they're welcome to it." He sucked on the end of his drooping brown mustache and added, "Him now, he don't look like he'd be much—his pants hangin' slack

and his shoulders humped worse'n my granddad's. But her!
You'd have to see her, Rolfe. What she's got ain't anything a
man could put words to."

As soon as Gus finished his coffee and started back to town
in his buggy, my mother mixed a batch of bread. "We'll take
over a couple of loaves and a cake," she said. "A woman
deserves better than that dirt-roofed cabin on the flats."

My Uncle Rolfe stood looking out the kitchen window. He
was big and handsome in a wild, blackheaded way. He was
always splitting his shirts and popping off buttons, and he
never cared what he had on or how it fitted. Uncle Rolfe
came to live with us and take over part of the ranch when my
father died, and you'd never have thought he was my mother's brother, for she was small and neat and had pale brown
hair.

"Anne," Uncle Rolfe said, "I wouldn't be in a hurry to rush
over and welcome a couple of squatters. We don't know
anything about them and they don't come from much when
they have to put up in a dead man's shack on the flats. What's
more, they won't stay long."

The color flew high in my mother's cheeks. "You don't
understand about a woman," she said. "You don't know how
much it helps to have a friend of her own kind in this big
lonesome country. You've been a bachelor too long to see a
woman's side of things, Rolfe Annister."

"Well," he said, "I aim to leave them alone."

But the next morning when we were ready to go, Uncle
Rolfe got in the buggy. "Won't hurt me to meet them, I
guess." Then he turned to me and smiled. "Billy, you want to
drive this morning?"

I was thirteen that spring morning in the mountain country, and nothing ever sounded better than the clop-clop of
the horses' hoofs and the singing sound of the buggy wheels
turning along the dirt road. The meadowlarks were whistling
and Uncle Rolfe began humming under his breath, the way
he did sometimes when the sky was soft and the grass coming
green.

It was six miles to the homesteader's cabin and we were almost there before we saw it, for it sat low on the flat land among the sagebrush and was the same silver-gray color. The river ran past it but there weren't any trees along the water, only a few scrubby willows still purple from the fall, for they hadn't leafed out yet.

First thing we noticed was the color in the windows of the old cabin, big blossoms of red and pink and white. My mother stepped out of the buggy and stared. "Geraniums!" she exclaimed. "I never saw anything so beautiful!"

The two-wheeled cart was beside the door and so old and bleached it might have been part of the land. And we saw the horse picketed in the sagebrush. Like Gus had said, he was a pack of bones with a belly slung down like a hammock.

My mother carefully carried her box with the cake and bread to the front door and knocked. She was wearing her new gloves, the ones Uncle Rolfe had bought her in Denver when he shipped the cattle.

The door opened slowly and all I saw that first moment was the woman's eyes, big and dark and shining. She was young and her hair was so blond it looked almost white and was drawn back tight until it made her eyes seem larger and blacker. She was brown-skinned and tall and she looked strong. Her dress was clean but so worn my mother would have used it for a rag.

"I'm Anne Studer," my mother said. "We're your neighbors. This is my brother, Rolfe, and my son, Billy."

The woman seemed to forget my mother and Uncle Rolfe. She bent over and put her hand on my head and smiled down into my face. "Billy," she said, and her hand stroked my head and I could feel she loved me, for the warmth came right out of her hand.

She asked us to come in and then I saw the bed on the floor near the stove and the man there in the blankets. His face was thin and gray and he sat up, coughing. "Sam," she said, "we've got company—our neighbors."

He didn't try to get up but just lay there, and I thought how terrible it was he didn't have any bunk or bedstead, only the floor under him. Then he smiled at us and said, "The trip was too much for me, I guess. We've come a long way. Melora, will you put on the coffee?"

The woman went to the old stove that had pools of velvety-looking rust on the lids and she set a small black pot on it and filled the pot with water from the bucket. Her arms were soft and rounded but strong lifting the bucket.

No one said anything for a few moments and I could hear a rustling that seemed to come from all the corners of the room.

"You've got lots of mice," my Uncle Rolfe said.

Melora smiled at him. "I know. And we forgot to bring traps."

Mother looked around and drew her skirts close to her, her mouth pinching into a thin line. I saw her touch the shiny lid of a tin can with her toe. The can lid was nailed over a hole in the rotting wooden floor.

Melora cut the cake, saying what a beautiful cake it was, and glancing at my mother, who still had that tight look on her face. Then she poured coffee into two battered tin cups and three jelly glasses. "Billy," she said to me, "if I'd been expecting you, I'd surely have fixed lemonade and put it in the river to cool." She stroked my head again and then walked over to one of the geraniums and I could see her fingers busy among the leaves. Her hands moved so softly and quietly in the plant that I knew she was loving it just as she had loved me when she touched me.

We didn't stay long and Melora walked to the buggy with us. She shook my mother's hand and said, "You were good to come. Please come back soon—and please bring Billy."

Driving home, my mother was silent. Uncle Rolfe finally said, "I knew we shouldn't go there. Makes a man feel low in his mind to see that. He's half dead, and how are they going to live?"

"I'm going to ride over with mousetraps," I said. "I'll set them for her."

My mother gave me a strange look. "You're not going alone," she said firmly.

"No," my Uncle Rolfe said. "I'll go with him."

A few nights later we rode to the house on the flats and Uncle Rolfe set twelve mousetraps. Sam was in bed and Melora sat on an old spike keg, her hands folded in her lap. We'd just get started talking when a trap would go off and Uncle Rolfe would take it outside, empty it, and set it again.

"Sam's asleep now," Melora said. "He sleeps so much—and it's just as well. The mice bother him."

"Isn't there any other place you can go?" Uncle Rolfe asked, a roughness in his voice. "You can't live off this land. It won't grow anything but sagebrush."

"No, we haven't any other place to go," Melora replied, and her strong shoulders sagged. "We've no kin and Sam needs this climate. I've got more plants coming from Missouri—that's where we used to live. I'll sell my geraniums. We'll manage—we always have."

She walked out in the night with us when we were leaving. She put her arm around me and held me hard against her. "So young," she said, "so alive—I've been around death a long time. Sam—look at Sam. And our babies died. We had two. And now, now I'll never have another child—only the geraniums." Her voice broke and I knew she was crying. Her arms swept me closer and there was something about the way she clung to me that made me hurt inside.

"Come on, Billy," Uncle Rolfe said gruffly. I pulled away from Melora and got my horse. I could still hear her sobbing as we rode away.

We were riding quietly in the dark when my Uncle Rolfe began to talk to himself, as though he'd forgotten I was there. "Beautiful," he said, "and needing a strong red-blooded man to love her. Needing a child to hold in her arms—and there she is, tied to *him*. Oh Lord, is it right?"

A week later my Uncle Rolfe wrapped a piece of fresh beef in a white sack and rode off toward the flats. My mother watched him go, a frown on her forehead. Then she said to me, "Billy, you bring in the milk cows at five o'clock. I don't think your Uncle Rolfe will be back by then."

The next morning I saw a pink geranium on the kitchen table and a piece of brown wrapping paper beside it. On the paper was written in strong sloping letters, "For Anne from Melora."

It wasn't long till everybody in the valley spoke of the cabin on the flats as "Geranium House." On Sundays, before the haying season started, the ranchers drove out in their buggies and they always went past the cabin on the flats. The women stopped to admire the flowers and usually bought one or two plants. They told my mother how beautiful Melora was and how kind—especially to the children.

"Yes," my mother would say and get that pinched look about her mouth.

One morning in early August when Gus brought the mail, he told us Melora had been driving all over the valley in the cart, selling geraniums and visiting with the women. "And she's got a new horse to pull the cart," he said, "a big black one."

That afternoon my mother saddled her horse and taking me with her went riding through the horse pasture. "I'm looking for the black gelding," she said. "Seems to me I haven't noticed him around lately."

We rode until sundown but we didn't find the gelding. I said he might have jumped the fence and gotten out on the range or into one of the neighbor's pastures.

"Yes," she said, frowning, "I suppose he could have."

She asked Uncle Rolfe about the black gelding and Uncle Rolfe let on like he didn't hear her. "Well," my mother said tartly, "there's such a thing as carrying goodwill toward your neighbors too far."

"You haven't," he said angrily. "You never bothered to go back. And she must be lonely and tired of looking at a sick man every day."

"She hasn't returned my call," my mother said, her chin in

the air. "I'm not obligated to go there again. Besides, there's something about her—the way she looks at Billy—"

"You've forgotten, Anne, what it is to hunger for love, for a child to be part of you—for a man's arms around you in the night."

Tears came into my mother's eyes. "No, Rolfe! I haven't forgotten. But I've got Billy—and when I saw her eyes and her hands on the geraniums——Rolfe, it isn't that I don't like her. It's—it hurts me to be around her."

Uncle Rolfe put his hand on her shoulder. "I'm sorry, Anne. I shouldn't have said a word."

"If she comes here," my mother said, "I'll make her welcome, Rolfe."

And then one warm morning I saw the two-wheeled cart driving up in front of the house, and I saw that the horse pulling it was our black gelding.

"Billy!" Melora called to me. "How are you, Billy?" And she got out of the cart and put her arms around me and I could feel the warmth coming from her body and covering me like a wool blanket in winter.

My mother came to the door and asked Melora in. "How's Sam?" she said.

Melora put her hand to her eyes as though she wanted to brush something away. She was thinner than when I'd last seen her and her eyes burned bigger and brighter in her face that now had the bones showing under the fine tanned skin. But still she looked strong, the way a wire is tight and strong before it breaks. "Sam," she said, "Sam's all right. As good as he'll ever be. It's a weakness, a sickness born in him—as it was in our babies. Anne, I didn't know Sam was a sick man when I married him. He never told me."

Uncle Rolfe came in with his black hair looking wilder than usual. The color burned in Melora's cheeks and her eyes lighted. "Hello, Rolfe," she said, "and thank you for being so kind to Sam."

"That's all right," Uncle Rolfe said gruffly.

"I went to town to see the minister," Melora said, still

looking at Uncle Rolfe. "I asked him to find me a baby I could adopt—like you suggested. He said 'no.'"

"He did!" Uncle Rolfe sounded shocked.

"He said I had nothing to take care of a baby," Melora went on. "He said I had my hands full now. I begged him to help me, but he just sat there with a face like stone and said it wasn't my lot in life to have a child."

"The fool!" Uncle Rolfe muttered.

My mother set food on the table and asked Melora to stay and eat with us.

Melora shook her head. "I'm going home and fix something for Sam. He can't eat much this hot weather but I tell him he must try. And he gets so lonesome when I'm gone."

My Uncle Rolfe went out and helped her into the cart. He stood for a long time looking down the road after she left.

Two weeks later we saw the buggy of Gus, the mailman, coming up the road. It wasn't the day for bringing mail. The horses were running and a big cloud of dust rose behind the buggy. My mother and I stepped onto the porch just as Uncle Rolfe rode in from the haying field with a piece of machinery across the saddle in front of him. My Uncle Rolfe dismounted and waited for Gus. The buggy rattled to a stop. The horses were panting and sweating, for it was a hot morning.

"Melora's taken Sadie Willard's baby," Gus said, "and drove off with it."

"Oh no!" My mother twisted her hands.

"Happened a little while ago," Gus said. "Sadie went to feed the chickens and when she came back she saw Melora's cart going over the hill in front of the house. She thought that was strange. She went in the house and looked everywhere and the baby was gone. She sent the sickle grinder to the hay field after Jim and just as I left Jim come in and said he'd get the neighbors and they'd go after Melora. It's a terrible thing and Jim's about crazy and Sadie sittin' cryin' like her heart would break."

Uncle Rolfe looked at my mother. "Anne, you take the lunch to the meadow at noon for our hay hands. Billy, you come with me." He jammed his big hat lower on his black head and we started for the barn.

The heat waves shimmered all around us on the prairie as we rode toward Geranium House. When we got there our horses were covered with lather, but there wasn't any sign of the cart or Melora. Everything looked still and quiet and gray except for the flowers blooming in the windows and around the outside of the cabin.

Uncle Rolfe pushed the door open and Sam was propped up on some pillows, reading an old newspaper. There were two bright spots of color in his thin cheeks. "Hello, Rolfe," he said. "Thought you'd be making hay."

"Where's Melora?" Uncle Rolfe asked.

"Melora? She left me a lunch and said she was going to drive up to the timber and get some water lilies. A lily pond she found a while ago, I guess. I don't know where it is, though."

"I do," Uncle Rolfe said.

"Folks are lookin' for her," I said, my voice rising with excitement. "I bet they're goin' to——" Uncle Rolfe's big hand covered my mouth and he shoved me toward the door.

"What's wrong?" Sam said. "Has something happened to Melora?" And his face twisted like he was going to cry.

"No," Uncle Rolfe said gently, "nothing's wrong with Melora. You just take it easy, Sam."

It took us a while to reach the timber, for it was so hot we couldn't crowd the horses and there was no wind moving to cool things off. The smell of pines was thick, almost clogging my nose, and I could see big thunderclouds building up behind the mountains.

I didn't know where the pond was but Uncle Rolfe rode right to it. It was a small pond and very smooth, with the blue dragonflies hanging over the yellow lilies. Uncle Rolfe got off his horse and I followed. He took a few steps and stopped, staring.

There sat Melora under an aspen tree, holding the baby against her breast and her eyes closed and her mouth smiling. She didn't look like any ordinary woman sitting there. She looked like the pictures of saints they have in Sunday school books.

Uncle Rolfe said, "Melora——"

She opened her eyes and looked at us. Then she said in a small frightened voice, "I only wanted to have him a little while to myself—to feel him in my arms. I meant no harm to him." She got up then, holding the baby carefully. "He's asleep and don't you bother him."

"They're looking for you," Uncle Rolfe said. "Melora, you shouldn't have done this. The women will never be your friends again."

Melora bowed her head and began to cry. The sun came through the trees and made her hair shine until it looked like a halo. "I only wanted to hold him," she said. "I only wanted to have him in my arms a little while."

"Hush!" Uncle Rolfe said roughly. "Where's the cart?"

"I hid it in the trees."

Then Uncle Rolfe took hold of her arm and said to me, "You bring the horses, Billy."

Melora cried all the way through the timber until we reached the cart. Then she sat stiff and quiet, holding the baby. I rode along behind, leading Uncle Rolfe's horse.

When we got to the cabin on the flats there were several buggies and saddle horses there, and men were standing by the front door, their faces dark and angry. Inside the cabin I could hear Sam shouting hoarsely, "She meant no harm, I tell you! She's good, a good woman with no mean thing in her!"

Uncle Rolfe took the baby and gave it to Sadie's husband, Jim Willard, and the baby wakened and started to cry. Jim Willard stared at Melora, his face ugly. "You get outta this country!" he shouted. "We've got no place for baby stealers in the valley. If you ain't gone by tomorrow night, I'll burn this shack to the ground!"

Melora shrank back, pressed against the wheel of the cart, her eyes filled with a terrible look of pain and her lips moving but no word coming out. The men began to mutter and shift restlessly and someone said, "Why don't we load their stuff and start 'em out of the valley now?"

Jim Willard kicked at one of the geranium plants that sat beside the cabin door. His big boot ground the blossom into the dirt. Melora gave a little cry and covered her face with her hands.

"That's enough, Jim!" Uncle Rolfe's voice was cold. He moved to stand close to Melora, his shaggy black head lifted, his fists clenched. "You men go home and leave her be. She's got no other place to go and her man's sick. I'll take care of things. I'll be responsible for her—and for him, too."

One of the men moved forward toward Melora and Uncle Rolfe's big hand grabbed him and shoved him aside, spinning him away like a toy man. There was some arguing then but Uncle Rolfe stood silent with that fierce look in his eyes. After a while the men got on their horses and in their buggies and went away. Melora walked slowly into the house and we could hear Sam half crying as he spoke her name, and then her voice, soft and warm, "I'm here, Sam. Now don't you fret. Sleep now, and when you waken I'll have supper ready."

"Come on, Billy," Uncle Rolfe said. His voice sounded old and tired. We rode slowly toward home.

It was black that night in the mountain country, black and sultry, the window curtains hanging motionless. When I went to bed it was too hot to sleep and I could hear thunder rumbling in the distance. Lightning began to play through the house, flashing streaks of blue and red, and I heard my Uncle Rolfe moving in the bedroom next to mine. I heard his boots on the floor and then his steps going to the kitchen and a door closing. I got out of bed and ran through the dark house and when the lightning flared again, I saw my Uncle Rolfe walking toward the barn. A little later, when the lightning glowed so bright it made me shiver, I saw my Uncle Rolfe ride past the window, his hat pulled low on his black head. He was headed toward the flats.

I was awake a long time, for it was hard to sleep with the thunder getting close and loud and the lightning popping all around. When the storm broke I got up again and closed the door of Uncle Rolfe's room. A little later my mother came into the kitchen and lighted the lamp and heated some milk for us to drink. We sat close together in the kitchen until the storm went over and a cool wet wind began to blow through the house.

I never knew when Uncle Rolfe got home that night but the next morning he was at the breakfast table. And all the rest of the summer he didn't ride toward the flats again.

It was far into fall and I was going to country school when Gus came one Saturday morning and brought my mother two large red geranium plants with the penciled message on brown wrapping paper, "To Anne with love, from Melora."

"Pretty," Gus said. "Never did see such geraniums as are in that house now. And Melora, she's bloomin' like the flowers."

Uncle Rolfe put down the local paper he'd just started to open and turned to look at Gus.

"Yes sir," Gus went on, "she always was a woman a man had to look at more than once, but now she's downright beautiful. Sam, he's not much better. Might be he'd die tomorrow and might be he'd live a few years yet. Never can tell about things like that. And I guess if he did die, somebody'd look out for a woman like Melora."

"I expect so," my mother said, pouring coffee for Gus.

"The Lord's favored her, make no mistake about that," Gus went on, "for she's going to have that baby she's been hankerin' for. The women, they've all forgive her for what she did and been up there with baby clothes and buyin' her geraniums again." Gus sighed and sucked at the end of his drooping brown mustache. "Only the Lord's doing would give a woman a baby when she needed it so bad and didn't have but a shell of a man to love her."

My mother lifted her head and stared at my Uncle Rolfe, a strange softness in her eyes and around her mouth. My Uncle Rolfe looked back at my mother and it seemed to me they said a lot of things to each other without speaking a word. Then my Uncle Rolfe opened the local paper and began to read the news.

THE PROMISE OF
THE FRUIT

ANN AHLSWEDE (1928–)

Author of three distinguished Western novels, Ann Ahlswede was born in Pasadena, California. Her ancestors went West during the gold rush and fought in the Civil War. It is that war which provides the background to "The Promise of the Fruit," Ahlswede's only short story. It was first collected in *The Pick of the Roundup* (1963). The story explores the devastating and inescapable guilt associated with war, both among those who participate in it and those who remain on the outside.

He came home from the big war with only one yearning in his heart. He was as tired as any soldier of the Confederacy, he wanted to put aside forever all the clever ways men taught themselves to kill each other; but most of all, after so long and so hard a journey, young Cullen Brace only wanted peacefulness.

He entered the roadway where he knew each twist, each path and dooryard, and the dust was fine and the echoes rang like distant, frail music to the ghostly fall of confetti, to the laughter of young girls and children, and in the crush of earth and blossoms beneath the boots of the outgoing soldiers:

We are a band of brothers, and native to the soil . . .

Full and rich in memory came his own voice lifted with strength and insistence in the rightness of it all. And in the green-scented darkness the night before leave-taking, Cullen Brace held Rachel and whispered to her, "You'll see! I'll come back when the fighting's over. No Yank'll ever kill Cullen Brace!" His whole body had been anguished with the sudden, piercing weight of love, and the burden of mortality, all felt whole, at once, as though he knew already what it was to die in battle, to love once in the rivergrass, experiencing only this and nothing beyond. Fervently he whispered to her, "I'll come home again!"

And he had, but never the way he had dreamed about it with her. His old boots stirred the dust in the awkward walk of a leg-wounded soldier with blue eyes and rough brown hair, and a stillness in his thinned, weather-aged face.

He stopped and stood bareheaded by the side of the road. The sun filtered down to him through the branches of a mulberry tree. In his nostrils was the smell of the dust and the papery smell of the leaves. He could almost hear the echoes coming sweetly again through the tarnish of time: *band of brothers . . .*

A dog barked. Cullen turned his head, shaking himself free of his reverie of the past as he looked outward to see and absorb all that he had hungered to see again, all things crowding into him sharp against his eyes and ears—the purple blossoms on the jacaranda tree by the hardware store; the willow brush tangle down by the river crossing; town dogs lazy in the shade; a woman's voice lifted to call a child. Over the length of his hungry body came the familiar hot-weather lethargy of a day in early summer, and from the tavern by the road in front of him seeped the smell of ale and grease and coffee and worn dry wood. Over his head the young fruit of the mulberry hung small from milky green stems, flushed with the wine of approaching ripeness, and bees worked among the weed blossoms by the curb at his feet.

He brushed at the travel dust on his ragged clothing, waiting for his mind to grow coolly shadowed with the certainty that the fighting was over at last, that he was finally home. He had walked from Missouri through Arkansas and on to this place by the river, this widening in the road. Before that he had ridden out of Texas when he should have died there after the trouble at Bonham. But he was still stubbornly alive as much by accident as any other man who had come through it all; and now he was home.

He straightened, ready, conscious of the clumsiness of his leg. Someday he'd be used to it, he supposed, and forget about it and step out expecting his leg to carry him easily as it always had. But it took a man a long time to give up part of himself even when he knew it was a fact. He even dreamed about running sometimes.

The pistol pressed against his body where he'd wedged it under his belt earlier in the day. The sudden fierce wave of loathing that rose in him at the thought of it was so intense, so violent, that he was sick and miserable with it. He yanked the pistol from his belt and stared at it. Ugly thing, death and destruction, no way to count its terrible toll. It stood for everything he was finished with and wanted to forget, everything that blackened his soul; because there had to be a time when men walked without death in their hands, there had to be a choice between that and the black, blind destiny of worms.

He looked around him, searching for a place. He looked up into the tree and found the fork, and laid the gun up there where the leaves and the shadows and the hanging fruit almost hid it. Let the gun grow rusty and forgotten, let the tree smother it until it was gone.

The planks of the walk were hot beneath the soles of his boots. An old granny woman shuffled past in front of him. His smile began in the faintest recognition but she went by without looking up, a lump-filled gunnysack clutched to her breast. Roots and greens from the riverbank and the meadows and the swamps, he thought, with a quick, dark pity for the woman. Food for hungry people without recourse, the poultices of the earth for the old and ailing and the defeated. Her dim eyes stared down vacantly to each feeble step as she rustled through the curb weeds and out into the afternoon sunlight.

He started on, and stopped again when two boys bolted by, jolting him backward. He caught at an awning post to keep from falling, and looked after them, at their quick legs, at the fishing poles they carried down to the river, at the hound dogs trailing languidly.

The planks vibrated as others passed, and no one noticed him in his old clothes and his boney hunger because there were still thousands of others like him wandering the long roads, old young men with the same look in their faces. He wanted to say, I'm home. I belong here. But he went on into the shade of the tavern, feeling foolish with so much hidden gladness.

The shadowed inner stillness of the room wrapped around him soothingly. Motes of dust hovered in the quiet light. His body seemed to part them like dry waves as he limped slowly to the bar, and stopped. He reached down into his gritty pocket, searching out the last coin saved for this.

A celebration, a triumph without a name. Glory Hallelujah! I'm home! He wanted to spend his coin grandly on one cool drink.

"Beer!" he ordered. The coin rang brightly on the wooden bar.

"Young Cullen Brace, ain't it?" the innkeeper asked. "Widow Brace's boy?"

"Yes sir?" Cullen answered. He did not recognize this man with one arm gone, but he grinned because this man had recognized him.

"Don't you all remember old Ed Zoel, boy?"

"Zoel?" Cullen echoed. Then laughter bubbled up inside of him and he saw the same kind of crazy, wild mirth twist Ed Zoel's mouth into a grin. "Ed Zoel," Cullen marveled, because he had not thought of Ed Zoel in all the years and now he was back, and Ed Zoel was back too.

"Yes sir," Zoel answered triumphantly. "It's me all right. I made it too."

Sighs and sniffling and throat clearing came from the far corner of the room where two old men haggled softly over the pawns on a chess board. The corner was dim as twilight. Cullen turned his head to stare at them, seeing bent spines and white, tufted hair and withered hands reaching out to touch the pawns with such anxiety that life and death hovered over the board, and each breath was a shallow jealous effort. Time dribbled away between their withered fingers.

Cullen turned his back on them again, suddenly angry.

It was like looking into a room closed away from life for a century. Like looking into a darkened, tarnished mirror filled with unwanted images.

In a twist of savage bitterness he hated the old men because they were so substanceless, so horribly invisible in the midst of life.

He, Cullen Brace, had fought to come home; he had bled, he was filled with the blood and pain of living, and it throbbed insistently through him with each stubborn heartbeat, making him live on with the sting of its pricelessness.

He would not see himself in the old men; he could not believe that life could be so pastel; so filled with melancholy patience. Time could never be so meaningless, no, by God, not to him, or the others like him who had suffered so much just to draw another breath.

He sighed, letting the anger drain away, telling himself to drink the beer and forget the rest. But he thought of Ed Zoel, with an arm lost. Hadn't he once shod Cullen's horse over at Jackson's smithy? How could he shoe a horse now, how could he ever go back to what he was once, whole and strong and full of humble purpose?

And why was the old granny woman out foraging in the fields? Was there no one left to take care of her? A morbid picture of his own mother came into his mind. He imagined her, before she died, grubbing and digging in the dirt for the roots in the earth.

Think of better things, he told himself. Forget all that and think of something good, something cool and filled with end-less peace . . .

Go down to the river and wash in the green water, wash away the stink of war; remember when you had a pole and bobber, and went barefoot in the mud, carefree in the world . . . ?

"Things is changed," Ed Zoel said. He tucked a glass under the stump of his right arm and held it there while he dried it with his left hand. He tipped his head back to look up at the ceiling beams, where dusty cobwebs looped down motionless in the hot air. He entered a dark and thoughtful contempla-tion of change with bitterness and wonder so old that it no longer showed in his moist, softening features. "Yes sir, things do change."

The stirring of light and air told Cullen that someone had entered the tavern from the afternoon outside. He drank his beer and remembered the river, miles of green banks and softly flowing water; he thought of the boys fishing there in the summer haze.

"You're in early," Ed Zoel said.

"I don't mind," a woman's voice answered. She walked around the end of the counter and lifted a shawl from her shoulders, leaving them chalky white in the gloom. She wore a faded dress of lavender satin that flashed garishly with each movement of her body. Her hair was the maple red of fall leaves. Cullen turned his head and looked at her hair and at her face, and the shock reached him slowly through his good dreams. "Rachel—?"

Her red curls swung as she turned to look at him, a smile on her lips. Then recognition froze the smile. She seemed to shrink before his eyes until the lavender satin hung loose over her small breasts and the hot black stockings sagged over her knees.

"Look who's home, Rae," Ed Zoel said to her.

Cullen pulled up straighter at the bar, reaching to his full height, balancing to make up for his crippled leg. Still he did not feel tall enough, not as tall and tree-straight as he once had been. But as he waited for her to say the first word and the excitement grew with tumbling thoughts and emotions, he saw the dress and understood what it meant. Seconds late with his comprehension, he stared at the dress and the dark blood flushed into his face. "What're you doing, what're you wearing that thing for?"

Rachel Danton straightened pridefully. The silence strained between them as she stood there in the ugly hurdy-gurdy dress and glared back at Cullen Brace as though she thought herself something rare, something marvelous to gaze at. Then her lips opened, red lips he'd kissed when they were only pink. "Well, so the big war hero comes home at last. Well, I declare!" Her high heels clacked against the floor as she walked closer to him. Her eyes gleamed like jewels in the merciful light which made her white face seem wonderfully alluring. "Well, I declare," she cried, for all the world to hear her astonishment. "Look who's here! It's Cullen Brace come home again like a poor lost sheep!"

"I see you didn't wait for me, Rachel Danton!"

"Wait?" she cried in wonder. "Wait forever?" An edge of misery crumbled her voice. "Wait forever like I had a thousand years to live, Cullen Brace? Wait while I lost everything I ever had and went hungry and . . ."

She broke off and turned sharply away from him as two men entered the tavern and stepped up to the bar, bringing silence into the room with them.

The old ones in the corner fretted over their game. Ed Zoel served beer to his customers, lifting his glance aimlessly over the room.

The bitter thoughts seethed through Cullen's mind.

It was the least a woman could do while her man was off. The least. Just wait.

But who could wait forever, like she said?

Like they all had a thousand years to live, and there was no hurry?

Like he hadn't changed, himself, and hadn't done things he was ashamed of?

Oh God, yes! Things he was ashamed of.

All right then. He had to tell her he wanted to understand all this; more than anything he wanted to understand, and not let other things matter—nothing in all the world but Rachel Danton and Cullen Brace, off in the clinging search for what they had once known.

"Oh, you righteous man," she accused in a bitter whisper. She leaned toward him from behind the bar, and their faces were close, and he forgot everything he wanted to say to her, every fearful, eager hope, every tenderness, for the brittle words spilled too quickly from her mouth. *"You saint! You sinless boy.* Your ma's dead, you know that? You know she died all alone on the farm like some poor old sick creature with no one to look after her and no one even knowing, and the land's gone now—"

"Rachel . . ." he began, and the morbid picture of his mother came back again, filled with shadow and abandonment.

"No, you listen for once, Cullen Brace!" Rachel cried.

"I know she's dead."

"You don't know everything, you—"

"Leave be, can't you? I know she's gone!"

"But you're too late now, too late for me, too late for her, too late for everything!"

"She died before it was over, I didn't even hear till six months later!" The blood throbbed hotly in his face with the injustice of her accusation. "If I'd walked down that road the day Lee surrendered it wouldn't have made her rise up out of her grave, Rachel Danton!"

"It's been a year, a whole year—and I stood in that doorway watching, and I looked for you with the ones that came down that road, and you weren't ever there, you just never came!"

"I couldn't get back. . . ."

"Why not?" She slashed the words at him triumphantly. "Because you'd been off burning and murdering with that Quantrill? Oh, don't look so surprised, Cullen Brace. We heard. Is that what you were doing, soldier boy? Running wild? Is that why you didn't get home till now?"

He was aware of the others in the room listening to each word. He could hear how this would sound to them now when it was all over, and easy to look back on, because if there'd ever been any glory shining from Quantrill's name in the early days, it had died forever into the butcher deeds of a man the Confederacy wouldn't honor with a commission, who made his war a personal vendetta and cut his way through Lawrence, Kansas, in search of enemies; and on to Baxter Springs in '63 and then south in flight into East Texas and the last bitter pretense of a soldier's war at Bonham. . . .

Oh yes, there were things Cullen Brace was ashamed of.

"Look at you," Rachel's voice broke across his bleak memories. Her eyes searched over him for all the newness, all the brightness he had once possessed. Suddenly she clawed at the paint on her own face. "Look at me!" She flung her hand out in a gesture of misery. "Look at this place—look at everything!"

At the end of the bar Ed Zoel polished a glass and looked idly up at the rafters. The old men paused in their game, foolishly bewildered by the intrusion of wretchedness not their own. The two customers, caught innocently in this scene, finished their drinks and walked out into the afternoon once more.

"But the fighting's over," Cullen Brace said to Rachel. He spoke the vital words he had nourished in his own heart, he offered them to Rachel, the highest of his hope, the best of himself. "The fighting is done with."

Rachel laughed.

"And a man don't need to carry weapons in his hands," he insisted stubbornly, blindly, because he would not believe in her disbelief.

"Don't he?" she countered. "Is that what you think down in your heart?"

"Yes ma'am, I believe it. Because it's so."

"You and your notions. Notions don't change things from what they are. All those notions don't turn dirt into dreams."

His mouth tightened, aging his face with a harsh, enduring expression. "You think I don't know what's real? Maybe I don't have half a leg left? Is that just a notion too?"

"Half—" she faltered. For an instant she looked child-young and woundable beneath the mask of paint. Her eyes rounded and glittered with a rush of tears. "You never said . . . oh my, you never said."

He caught her hand, his face lighting with new eagerness. "Oh, I didn't mean to go and make it sound that bad. It ain't off or anything, it's just lame. It gives me fits, sometimes."

She looked searchingly into his face, the tears pooled in her eyes. "You are so thin."

Her hand was tight and warm in his, a lifeline grasp straining between them. He waited, all age and harshness drained from his face in the eagerness and the anxiety of his waiting.

"You say it's over," she said. The tears spilled quietly down over her cheeks. Her lips were wooden with the effort for control. "Make me believe it then. Make me believe it too."

The tavern doorway darkened suddenly.

Rachel looked past Cullen's shoulder. All at once her expression hardened again. Before Cullen's eyes she became too wise, too unbelieving.

"Oh no, Cullen Brace. No, it just ain't so!" Angrily she pulled back from him, drawing away when he would have held her and weakened her with his belief.

"Why?" he demanded. "Why ain't it so?"

She laughed again. "Because here comes that Tooley Jackson looking to shoot you."

Tooley Jackson was a great, strong man in the very prime of his life. There were streaks of premature gray in his hair. Lines of past hardships made his face almost ugly, so bold and open were they for the world to see. His mouth was large and calm, his nostrils wide, his dark eyes burning with some great purpose. He stood in the doorway with the afternoon light bright behind him, and stared at Cullen while quiet deepened in the tavern.

"I'm looking for a feller calls himself Cullen something-or-other," Tooley Jackson said. His mouth formed a single word with care. "You?"

Cullen looked around uncertainly. He frowned, because Rachel's words made no sense to him. The worry line deepened between his brows. "Yes sir," he answered. "That's my name."

"You the boy that rode with Will Quantrill?"

Cullen felt a coldness sink into him. He looked around at the others again, wondering what all this meant, where it was taking him. He saw that the room had begun to fill with people, people he had known all his life, and he heard not one greeting and saw no smile of recognition. He hesitated, bewildered by the silent weight of their hostility.

"Well?" Jackson spoke the round, full word quietly.

Cullen looked at Rachel. He answered, "Yes sir. I guess I rode with him."

A tremor passed over Tooley Jackson's face. "You one of them plundering killers who called theirselves *Irregulars?*"

"No sir, I was a *soldier,*" Cullen answered quickly.

"You one of them loyal boys who robbed their own and killed their own for the money and the pleasure of it?" Tooley Jackson's voice grew louder with each breath, thundering across Cullen's answer.

"No, listen to me . . ."

"You one of the four hundred that raided in Kansas?"

"No!"

"Them that looted Lawrence and massacred every man there?"

"I wasn't at Lawrence, I joined up afterwards!"

"You rode with Will Quantrill, didn't you?" Tooley Jackson shouted. "Didn't you?"

"Yes I did! But not at Lawrence!"

"You rode with him!"

Cullen's mouth was suddenly cotton dry. He looked

around, tearing his stare from Jackson's; he looked into Ed Zoel's empty face, and beyond to the two old men who had stopped their game to gape uncomprehendingly. He saw the young boys push through the circle closing around him, back from the river and the afternoon's whim. He saw Rachel, and all the others, watching, listening all around him.

A hunger like that of starvation moved in his body, a hunger to be heard, to tell someone. "Listen . . . will you just listen? I never raided at Lawrence, my God no. I was a soldier. When we attacked Helena in Arkansas I got hit in the leg. It was July of '63." The words spilled out, reaching out to these people, this great bitter man. "They started to cut off my leg right then but I said no, like hell they would, and then they told me if I didn't die anyway I'd be all through with the war afterwards." He felt their eyes go down to his legs, prying and hunting for the long, ugly scars. "There was a war on yet," he explained urgently. "Only I couldn't fight it anymore and there wasn't anything else, nothing but fighting, that's all there was. Just fighting and being scared of getting killed or torn up in some stinking shell burst, or being caught and put in Rock Island Prison. Or losing, like we hadn't fought with everything we had." He paused breathlessly because this was so terribly important. They had to understand how it was to be left useless with a cause still burning in your heart. Had they forgotten, themselves? Had they never felt the wrath in defeat? "I was sick with my leg," he went on, trying to strike through their stony silence to the things that were common in all of them. "I don't remember where I was, I just kept walking. I couldn't go fast. There wasn't any place to stop. It didn't make sense. I kept thinking we were really losing, like some people said, I kept thinking all the dying'd been *wasted*."

He stopped at last, dismayed, failing, exposed, for he had bared the melancholy in his own soul. But the people only watched him coldly. None of this mattered. He wet his lips. His anger was deep and chagrined. "All right! Maybe that don't matter, maybe yes and no is all you want to hear.

Quantrill raided Lawrence in August, didn't he? Well I heard
about it afterwards and then that Yankee General Ewing put
out the order that burned the Missouri border to get back at
Quantrill for going into Kansas."

"There was Southerners in Lawrence too," Tooley Jackson
challenged.

"I don't know nothing about Lawrence!" Cullen answered.
"Will you let me tell it?"

"I already know all I need to know."

"You asked did I ride with Quantrill and I'm telling you
why!" He waited, glaring at Jackson and the others. They'd
asked and now he'd make them listen. "So I set out looking
for Quantrill. He was still fighting. It took me a month because I couldn't walk fast but I went on looking because he
was *still fighting.* It was a way to keep on. That's why I rode
with him, only I didn't join up until the end of September.
After Lawrence!"

"You lie."

"I don't lie, I'm telling you true only you won't listen. I
joined him just before Baxter Springs!"

"What about Bonham, Texas?"

"I was laid up with my leg again after we went into Texas. I
rode with him at Baxter Springs against a Union detachment
—against soldiers! But before God I never raided in Texas
with the others."

"Listen to him," Tooley Jackson cried. "Talking himself out
of all the wrong." His eyes glittered with the hard tears of
grief and anger. "We was a sizeable family but the war took
us down right off at Bull Run and Cedar Mountain. Then Will
Quantrill came looking for that Yankee Red-Leg senator Jim
Lane, and Lane ran out the window and hid in the woods,
then Quantrill killed every man and boy he could find, every
one! He shot my old pa and he shot my two brothers and he
shot my only boy, while I was off to the fighting, and now I'm
all that's left. I'm the last one."

The silence was grieved, shared, weighted with debt.

"But I wasn't there," Cullen said to them. He looked around, begging for belief. "I wasn't even there!"

"You are a stinking Quantrill butcher and I am going to kill you now," Tooley Jackson said. "Get ready."

Cullen stared at the others, stunned by the suddenness of this. "D'you believe him?" he asked them furiously. "Is this what you want? What're we supposed to do, kill each other?" He paused, panting. *"Why?* What good'll it do now, what's it supposed to prove? He kills me and I kill him and what's left? What's it mean? That it just keeps going on till there's nobody left?" He waited for an answer but they only watched him, their faces blunt, secretive, dull with what seemed like a great weariness of mankind itself, a great indifference. Cullen felt cold, abandoned; he felt as though he were the last man on earth. "This ain't the war at all," he charged them bitterly. "What d'you want me for! Ain't you had enough yet?"

Tooley Jackson answered him quietly, "I am no big gun-fighter and I never fought a duel nor killed a man except on the line like any soldier following orders. But I know I'll make out today because it's a debt that's owed me, it's a justice."

"You going to kill them all?" Cullen asked with a wild twist of mirth. He laughed. "All four hundred men who rode into Lawrence?"

"I'll start with you."

"No sir. I won't fight you!"

Silence seeped through the room like a gray, chill mist. Coward, it said. Yellow coward. "I wasn't there," Cullen repeated. He pointed at Tooley Jackson and spoke to the others. "I don't even *know* him! I never killed his people. I never made war on anybody but soldiers! Now he stands there wanting to make a fight, dying to kill me, and he's wrong! He's wrong. It's all for nothing." They did not answer him and he shouted, "Can't you hear? Can't you talk?" Still he saw no flicker of response, no willingness. His hand dropped to his side as he began to believe that nothing he said would matter. "I won't fight him!"

Tooley Jackson said, "Then I will purely shoot you down where you stand."

Cullen's heart beat rapidly. How could this be what he had returned to when he had come searching for things far from the streams of chaos and calamity?

He felt the force of their waiting silence. He scarcely believed all this was happening to him.

He had dared to hope for work to do and food to eat and peacefulness, and moments to stand in idle contemplation beneath a mulberry tree and smell its greenness, and look forward to its summer fruit.

Now Tooley Jackson would shoot him where he stood and maybe he wouldn't ever feel the bullet, and no one would stop it; then later they'd lay him out in his rags and bury him prayerlessly on the graveyard hill.

Their waiting hurried him in his floundering thought. How could you set out to try to kill a man you didn't know when you'd sworn you were done forever with all of that, sick to death of it all, seeing its pointlessness? Clinging to a last tenacious faith even when your own ignorance and uncertainty overwhelmed you—

"You want to die like a dog?"

"I don't want to die any way at all!"

"Make your choice."

"You're wrong, you're wrong. . . ."

"Make your choice!"

Cullen looked into Ed Zoel's passive face, searching, appealing, waiting for some word. But all he saw was the wonder of time and change. Beside him were the two old men drifting effortlessly, unimportantly toward death. And only a step beyond in the living circle were the boys, a curious innocence in their faces as they watched and did not understand, and waited to be shown.

Cullen wanted to run; he wanted to close his eyes and open

them, and find that this was only a nightmare rising cruelly out of the travail of war.

But he remembered that he could not run anymore, that each step he took was now and forever more an effort of will, and pain, and hardheaded faith.

A breeze outside rustled the leaves of the mulberry, a breath of river coolness brushing across the heat of the afternoon laden with the spice of meadows and pines and sunlight.

"I am through waiting," Tooley Jackson said.

Cullen straightened. His throat felt thick, and he cleared it and said the soft, hollow words. "I left my weapon outside."

"Then let's get to it."

The crowd followed at his back as he entered the afternoon again. The day seemed strangely unchanged, as though no time had passed.

He limped to the tree and reached up through its leaves to the fork. His fingers touched the gun even as he breathed the greenness of the leaves and the bittersweet promise of the fruit. He hesitated. He tore one of the berries loose and put it in his mouth. A flood of sourness came from the unripe fruit. It was too soon; too green. He had known it. Yet ripeness hovered; the taste, the promise, lingered hauntingly.

He limped out into the open of the roadway. He stood there, looking at the Goliath figure of Tooley Jackson. He could not believe it was happening, and yet he knew.

The fighting is over, he had told Rachel with such certainty. It has to be sometime.

But when? When!

His own faltering shook him; he was more afraid than he had ever been.

Make me believe it, too, Rachel Danton had begged him.

He squeezed his fingers around the grips of the old gun, torn with a last urgent indecision. The muscles of his hand contracted with paralyzing tightness.

Make me believe it.

I . . . But I came so far. . . .

A spurt of fear shot all through him then as he saw Tooley Jackson move, and the time diminished to nothing and he thought wildly, I can't, I can't!

In all of Cullen's life no sound was so loud as the thunder of Tooley Jackson's shot. He heard it as he felt the great bewildering blow of the ball striking him, and the thundering blast surrounded him and lifted him, and he fell brokenly, his limbs awkward in the dirt of the roadway. He did not know if he had fired the gun; in the waves of shock he didn't know. He tried to get up again but his limbs were oppressively burdened, his movements grotesque. He fell back and tasted dust in his mouth and saw it in his eyes; he saw the sky beyond, far above him.

One by one the faces came to peer down at him. He saw the people he had known all his life. They stared, and still their silence was unbroken as they watched him breathing desperately. He waited to see Tooley Jackson there among them because the wrongful debt wasn't yet paid in full. Urgently he tried to remember if he had fired his gun; he had to know this. His fingers moved in the dust, searching feebly, finding only themselves in the granules of earth; his hand was empty. He could feel his hand's vast emptiness.

"Why didn't you shoot it, boy?" Ed Zoel asked from the circle above him.

Cullen did not try to answer him. The relief streamed flooding clean and bittersweet all through him, as sweet and bitter to his spirit as the juices of the unripe berries had been to his mouth.

But up there against the blue of the sky the faces of the two boys looked down at him, and the sweetness died, crushed, a terrible agonized loss; only the bitter remained. Because maybe this was the end of their last innocence with the sight and the stink of blood running out in the dirt.

At last he saw Tooley Jackson again. The great man loomed so high and so far above that he shut out the sky from Cullen, and dwarfed the people in his towering rightness.

Pain began to reach Cullen's brain. He struggled in the ultimate wonder of whether Tooley Jackson would fire again, because he did not know even yet if a man could live on without a weapon in his hand, although he knew how marvelously easy it was for a man to die weaponless, with only a longing for peacefulness clutched in his fists.

"No," someone said from the circling faces above.

"No more," a dull voice insisted. "No more!"

"It's enough."

Tooley Jackson stared down at Cullen. The day went endlessly on with birdsong and the blooming of flowers and the blowing of wind while Tooley Jackson looked down at the man at his feet.

He lifted the gun again, and held in his palm the dark before Genesis, the dark of nothing.

Cullen waited for the answer. He felt nothing, and then he felt an innocence like that of the boys; then that too was gone.

"Oh damn you, boy," Tooley Jackson whispered at last. His long, shaking sigh was like the wind in the river trees, as thwarted, as lonely. He dropped the gun from his hand and let it lie there, near the place where Cullen's gun had fallen. His fingers held its shape in a lingering echo. Then that passed and he turned away. He parted the people with his hands. They moved aside and closed in after him once more, pressing and circling in a wall of flesh around Cullen Brace and his red place in the dust.

A passing warmth and abrasion touched Cullen's face. The boney fingers of an old man plucked at dirt embedded in the sweat and cold of his shock. He sensed a chaos of motion and sound all around him and above him, a restless stirring as though some paralytic isolation had been broken.

"Take him inside," a woman's voice pleaded. "Please. Let me take care of him now."

A piping boy's voice asked, "He going to die, Mr. Zoel?"

"No, damn it! No he ain't. Not now. Can't you see?"

The words lifted a helpless worry from Cullen. Relief flowed through him, because he had come such a long, hard way. He closed his eyes tiredly.

It wasn't just for nothing then, and that was a relief too. And maybe men like himself, and all the others, fools, heroes, men who dared to hope, maybe they were more than tearless, bloodless pawns played in a game they'd never understand. . . .

The light was yellow-bright against his lids. He felt quick hands grasp him in islands of feeling all along the awkward length of his body; children's hands, the hands of the old and the crippled, all of them straining, bearing up the burden.

THE DEEP VALLEY

LUCIA MOORE (1887–1983)

Lucia Moore was born in Eugene, Oregon, where her father had
been mayor. She and her two sisters wrote a history of their
hometown that was published in 1949. She won a Spur Award for
The Wheel and the Hearth (1953), a novel about a family's move
overland to Oregon. "The Deep Valley," which appeared in *The
Pick of the Roundup* (1963), is also set in Oregon. Concerned with a
Basque sheepherding family, it probes a relationship between a
father and his daughter that represents the conflict of old-world
values with the new way of life in the American West.

Giede Petrie rode his cayuse pony with light rein, a man
pleased with his world, serene. There was no worry in his
warm, dark eyes as they scanned the valley.

Wool Valley some called it and Giede, understanding the
reason, could smile. The land spread wide and deep around
him, white-dotted with the hundreds of fine merino sheep he
allowed to roam, circling to far hills.

Giede liked it that way, as his father before him had liked
the land in Spain's Pyrenees, for the hills shut away an America that Giede had never learned to comprehend, and they
kept Marta just for him, the way the hills had kept his mother
for his father, with no adventuring. By America's law Giede
and Marta owned their land together, but not in Giede's
mind.

In Giede's mind it was his, along with all of neighboring
Yonder Valley, and the hillsides, other valleys beyond the

hills, and the sheep that drifted everywhere. And the sun and moon and stars.

The narrow trail lay in silence but for the soft breath of leather and pad of pony feet. "You and me, Freckles," he said. "We roam happy, eh? This all, all ours." He stroked the cayuse with a hand as wrinkled as an old turnip too long in a root cellar. The skin of his face was of the same texture, browned by sun and wind of the high country and dry as summer's eastern Oregon land, and as hard to change.

But for all the calm look of him and the gentleness in his voice there was a trouble in Giede's heart—a new trouble. Things had come to a strangeness now that Drushella had got to sixteen and pretty and the changes, pleasant in a way, disturbed him as he watched his daughter, her bright head bent above the spinning wheel while she made strong and fast the threads for spinning, then wound them into balls for Marta's weaving. He would watch, listening for the laughter that never came now. Tomorrow would turn the threads into yellows of the dye pot—yellows from the sassafras bark that came from Texas, greens from the onion in the valley, red from the cochineal he brought from town. But what about those tomorrows for this daughter of his and Marta's? What would the spinning of days bring to her? And what the dyes? And the many threads not of his tending or of Marta's?

He stared ahead, and no longer saw the brightness of morning or the polka dots of sheep against high hills. He and Marta and this strange, alien land were the loom, the warp. But what of the shuttle? What of the yet unwoven pattern for their girl whose eyes were as Marta's—dark, with never any happiness in them but always now only a smoldering fire and always, always the vast lonesomeness of the forests beyond the river?

The worry in his mind had sharpened yesterday. He had been forced to listen to the woman talk that had, after all, come to be a part of his days. It was Drushella who questioned the need for so much spinning.

"Pa could just as well buy this goods. Habersham's had it almost as fine."

Marta's eyes sought out Giede's, then looked away. "The goods in Habersham's don't last." The spinning wheel whirred faster. "Our own are better, Dru."

Giede was surprised that Dru should know of Habersham's. She rode every day over the valley and the hills, it was true, but never to the town; neither she nor Marta had seen the main street by the Falls. It was a long way to the river, a day's ride for a woman who was safer at home where there was plenty to keep her busy; what with the tallow to make into candles to hang in the shed for drying; the soap to stir in the brass kettle, the glue to make, and the leathers to soften and tan. All the things that a good sheep rancher had to do. Giede was a good rancher; so good that he had lately bought many hundreds more animals, and he could see them now, cropping the fine grass of this valley land not his own. It did not worry him that in the far valleys men hated him for this cropping.

The sun was high, and he spurred Freckles to a quick trot. They dusted through the main street to Ketter's Drug Store, where he tied the cayuse at the one hitching post after loosening the reins to let the pony drink sparsely at the pump trough. He threw a worried look toward the druggist's signboard with its green pestle and mortar, then opened the small door. Somehow the day had deadened, the way it always did when he felt the town around him.

The druggist stood at his prescription desk, his gray head bent above the capsules he was filling from a squared mass of yellow powder. He dabbed one last capsule into the powder, capped it, and gave his attention to Giede.

"You out of your shell, Giede? It's been a spell since town saw you." He came out, maneuvering his wooden leg around the corner of the fine new glass showcase with its perfumes and bristle brushes. "How's your lonesome hills, anyway?"

Giede studied the counter. "They ain't lonesome, Ketter. This new?"

Ketter nodded, pointing to the bottles of perfume. "That girl of yours would like some. Violet, maybe. She must be growed up by now and ready for perfumery."

"She's growed up," Giede snapped. "All I want is sassafras tea, some of that red cochineal like last time, and six pounds of sulphur."

"All right, all right!" Ketter reached to a shelf for the tea and the dye. "If you want sulphur for a tonic you better take some of these capsules. They's a lot of trouble and bad taste saved."

Giede said, "Marta can stir up sulphur and molasses. She don't need trouble saved."

The druggist began to wrap the small packages. "Violets smell sweet on a girl," he sighed. "Like springtime."

"This ain't spring—" Giede was saying when the door opened.

The man who came in was young and lean and tall—a good six feet two, with an easy swing to him and a fresh sunburn that had only just begun to shade to brown. His hair was polished as dark leather and his quick smile lit up the place.

"You got some arnica, sir?"

Ketter's eyes fetched a glint of amusement as they went over the long, tight lines of the young stranger. "You don't look like a body that'd need arniky. But I've got it." He stumped over to the patent medicine shelf, wooden leg beating a tattoo. "Big size or little?"

"Better make it big," the man said. "I ache all over." His eyes met Giede's and there was a seriousness in them now. The two considered each other before Giede nodded.

"You new around these parts?" He was thinking, *Eyes blue as camas. Hair black as the face on that old ewe that broke her leg. Irish. Black Irish.*

"If getting here a couple of weeks ago is new."

That seemed to be the end to the answer, and Giede turned away pretending to study the calendar on the wall. He saw that it said June 15th and that it pictured the moon at first quarter.

Ketter thudded back with the arnica. "That'll cure a lot of charley horses. Did I hear you say you'd been here a couple of weeks?"

The man was going through his pockets for change. He tossed out a five-dollar gold piece. "Thereabouts."

Ketter kept at it. "Everybody gets around here sooner or later. But we ain't seen you."

The stranger's quick smile flashed. "Been busy getting lamed up. I got myself a piece of land and I'm not used to land."

"Well, now, you couldn't do better than to own land in Oregon," Giede interposed. "It's worth aching for. How much land?"

"Too much."

"I can't think what you mean by that," Giede said.

"Nothing special. This is tempting country and maybe I overdid it a little, that's all."

Ketter grinned. "That's youth for you." He was wrapping the arnica. "If it's finances that bother you—money you need —plenty of men around here can give it." He glanced at Giede, but Giede had gone back to studying the calendar.

"Money's not what I need, Doc. I reckon they do call you Doc, with all these bottles and pills?"

"Some do. Name's Ketter." He put out his hand.

"I'm Jon Arrow. Glad to know you, Mr. Ketter."

The druggist turned to Giede. "I can't think of anything we're lacking in Oregon Country but money and maybe fences. We got everything else." It was his turn to grin and the grin was for Giede. "Where you located, Mr. Arrow?"

The boy's dark head indicated the mountains to the east. "Between the hills. Yonder Valley they call it. As pretty as you could ask for, but the land's been run over by sheep! I bought it for cattle land." Bitterness weighted his face. "Six hundred acres of it!"

Giede's head jerked up. "The hell you say!" He met Ketter's startled look.

Jon Arrow was picking up his package. "Got any cure here,

Doc Ketter, for a man dumb enough to buy cattle land without seeing it?"

Ketter did not look at Giede this time. "Well, now, that depends. Fences cure some ailments." He chuckled. "You met your neighbor yet over in Wool Valley?"

"The son of a bitch! No! I've been seeing his sheep, though. And I'm waiting for him."

Ketter loosed a sly grin. "No need to wait. Meet Giede Petrie, mister."

The two faced each other, the one gimlet-eyed and with a face turnip-seamed; with shoulders bent from work but that straightened now in defense; the other taut, impatient to meet the man he already hated.

Giede made himself mutter "Howdy," taking the impact of Arrow's eyes. Then he said, "So I'm a son of a bitch."

Jon Arrow didn't speak for a full minute. The room grew tense before he said, "A man's got a right to his sheep. But not to all the acreage between Dan and Beersheba. Fences were made for sheep."

The gentleness of it surprised Giede Petrie. He spoke quietly. "Ever see a band of sheep jump a fence?" he asked.

"I can't say I have if the fence is high enough." Arrow turned around at the door. "Six feet ought to do it, Mr. Petrie." Then he was gone.

Ketter looked smug. "Well. Put that in your hair shirt an' scratch it."

Giede snorted. "Hair shirt, hell. My sheep are high-toned sheep. Best in this country, and as good as anybody's cattle." He took up the package of sulphur, tucked the tea and cochineal into his shirt pocket. "My sheep got their breed in Spain for my father before me."

"Spain or Wool Valley, you heard what he said about fences."

"It was you mentioned fences," Giede reminded Ketter. Then he remembered that he had promised to buy six yards of yellow cashmere from Habersham's. He hurried out, not waiting for what Ketter would say.

Two doorways separated Habersham's from Ketter's, one of them the louvered door of Midnight Jones' saloon. Giede didn't often go to Midnight's but now he pushed through the swinging doors. The place was almost empty. Midnight, black-eyed and with a band of dark whiskers like a baboon's, grinned as Giede slowed to the bar.

"Jest like a ole mole!" Jones finished shining a beer mug. "You come up again?"

Giede threw money onto the bar. "Fill that mug and give me a double whiskey, too." Giede never wanted a bottle in front of him and it was a notion that goaded Midnight.

He put the glass and mug in front of Giede. "I hear you ain't alone anymore out in your hills." He watched while Giede tipped the double whiskey down, sputtered, and began on the beer. It wasn't like Petrie to make a business of getting drunk.

Giede didn't hurry the beer. He contemplated the suds. "You can hear anything," he said. He didn't want to talk. Since the whiskey hit his stomach he wanted to think about Drushella and the yellow cashmere. A funny thing why she'd insisted on six yards of it. Yellow, at that, and hard to keep clean. Foolish as damned silk. Costly, too. And where was Dru going to wear a yellow dress when she'd sewed it up? He would ask her tonight, if it still seemed important. Maybe, at that, she would look pretty fine in yellow, with her bright hair like the brass along Midnight's bar. When he had finished the beer he could picture her, and he walked out and straight to Habersham's.

"Cashmere," he announced, nodding at the two Habershams. "Yellow." When it was unrolled he fingered it, catching a breath. It was fine stuff all right. "Six yards." When Habersham had hastily made the first cut into it Giede added three spools of thread to match and with a final big sweep of his hand two yards of the wide yellow ribbon he discovered in the showcase.

Mrs. Habersham came close. "My, my! That'll make a lovely sash for the dress." Giede was silent, pocketing the small change from a twenty-dollar gold piece and finding the door, his package hugged to him.

"Giede must be drunker than he looks," Habersham said, rolling away the bolt of bright cloth. "Used to be he'd see that Marta wove her cloth, according to his bragging."

Mrs. Habersham smiled happily. "That ain't for Marta, Shammy. That's for Drushella, and Giede had better tend his fences for sure now. Somebody's jumped 'em."

Her husband chuckled. "Fences he has not got, Mrs. Shammy, and fences he will not have."

She hugged herself, pleased with the sale and because Drushella would have a fine dress. "Maybe he'll rue the day, Shammy."

Giede, riding home groggily, was thinking the same thing. In spite of the first quarter moon it was pitch-black in the hill shadows as he rounded the bend opposite Yonder Valley and the land the upstart Arrow had come to. Another time he'd ride over and see what went on there. The skeleton of a deserted shack stood ghostlike in the thin moonlight and past it the Indian pony trotted faster while the night air stiffened.

By the time Giede saw his own log house, long and low to the hillside, he had pushed Jon Arrow far to the back of his thoughts. He hurried to unsaddle and turn the pony loose, took off his boots, and crept up the three steps and down the length of the narrow porch to the wool room. Here Marta carded the wool, and the room had a pleasant smell. He would sleep here tonight, because Marta knew too well when he'd had a drink. Content, he burrowed into the mound of wool.

It was two days before he rode away toward Yonder Valley, and they were pleasant days. He let them slip by, with Marta humming as she set the salt-rising yeast at the hearth, or stirred the fragrant rhubarb jam in the brass kettle in the barnyard. Marta had seemed to take no notice of his day away, nor cared that he had slept in the wool room, and he guessed that interest in the yellow cashmere had forestalled his trouble, with Drushella handily cutting, then sewing, the long seams. The cloth was as golden as the eaves of a poplar tree at autumn frost.

On the second evening Drushella said, "This will soon be finished, Pa." There was a pride in her voice but Giede pretended that he had not heard, staring out at the lowering sun. "Pa! I said my dress is almost finished!" She was holding it up, and he saw how well the stays had been sewn tight around the small waist of it.

"That the outside?" he asked, lacking anything else to say.

Drushella smiled. "Good gracious, no! I'd look pretty dancing with my stays showing!"

Marta, bending at the open fire, straightened slowly, sensing a crisis. Giede looked at her, then at his daughter.

"Dancing! Who says anything about dancing?" They were not just words. They were like fire crackling.

Neither woman answered.

"You heard me!" Giede got to his feet. He was trembling. "I said who's talking about dancing?"

Drushella's eyes were hidden from him, attention on her stitches. Without looking up she said, "I am, Pa."

A hard crust of silence held them all. Marta bent again to her cooking while the girl's needle thrust in and out, in and out. Giede's face had gone dark and cruel, but they didn't see. Then he broke the silence.

"There will be no dancing. You will hang that dress behind the curtain in the corner!" His big fist hit the table. "Gawd-a-mighty! Dancing! There will be no dancing. Never! Never!"

Marta straightened, pulling taut the tired muscles in her back. "*Never* has been a very long time, Giede, and you're a fool," she said quietly. She had never spoken so in all their lives before.

He wanted to strike her. Blind fury filled him. He faced her. "Never will be a longer time! Never! Never. Never. I say it." He clenched his fists as he whirled on Drushella. "You hear me?"

The girl looked up at him, her dark eyes smoldering. "I heard. And stop shouting at Ma. And at me. I will go dancing whether you agree or don't. Tomorrow night with Jon Arrow."

It was impossible for Giede to speak. His big hands worked, clenching and loosening, he could feel a sickness within him. It was Marta who tried to calm him in the way she always had.

"There is no harm in it, Giede. Jon Arrow that bought the ranch across the hills will come for her. It's square dancing in his new barn." Still Giede stared at them. "Jon is covering his land with Devon cattle. His barn is big—and fine—"

Giede's head snapped up then. "Barn! There is no barn! I passed by two days ago. There is the same old shack, nothing more. And there will be no dancing! Barn or no barn there will be no dancing!" He sat down slowly like an old man. "Look what you have done to me, Marta. I am old."

"You are an old man then at forty," Marta said.

Her complacency stung him. He forced himself to his feet. He would see whether there was a barn, whether there were cattle. He walked to the door, jerked it open, and strode out.

Bitterness ate at him as he saddled the cayuse pony. These hills that had shut them in would fail him now. If this girl of his went dancing even once, what good would the hills be to him? And how had it begun? Dru had been seeing this Jon Arrow, and Marta knew. Marta knew. A sharp-edged fear knifed at him. How could there be cattle, and how could Marta know about them? A week ago there had been nothing but cropped grass where the sheep roamed, fine grass. Always fine grass for them ahead. Grass blowing in the wind as far as a man could see. Grass Giede had counted on, the way he had counted on Marta and on Dru. He rode the dusty trail glowering at the sunset sky, at the lifting hills, uncomforted by them, and afraid.

After a time there lay the far valley, green and soft in the early evening, and he pulled the cayuse up. There was still no barn in sight. His keen eyes sought out every corner, every ravine. There was not even smoke from the mud chimney of the shack. "Ah!" he gloated. There was not one moving thing to see but the waving grass, and far off a thin cloud of dust that the wind had stirred up. He caught a deep breath, relieved and secure again, until he thought about the dancing. A girl would not lie about the dancing, seaming up a dress that she would never wear. Perhaps beyond the far hill a barn stood this minute. . . . He spurred the pony to a gallop.

In no time he saw it, a high, wide thing with open doors swung out from a great loft where hay, new-pitched, shone gold where the low sun struck it. But the barn was not the thing that held Giede's attention. Far up and along the rim of the hills a fence crept, to disappear beyond the slope. Sick at heart, Giede turned his pony.

It was then that he saw a cloud of dust spreading thick along the road to the west. Looking into the sun he saw it grow, come nearer, until the bawling of cattle reached his ears. He sat stunned, feeling his mountains fall away, his valley naked and no longer his own. After a while he rode back along the way, unsaddled, hung the saddle on its peg, stroked its leather gently. This leather he had taken from his own sheep, this leather Marta had tended, toned, shined, and watched him fashion into a saddle.

The evening had dropped far beyond the last hill. Giede crouched down in the corner of the friendly barn where he kept a blanket. The blanket smelled sweet with the soap that Marta had washed it in, and he lay alone, hearing the bells of sheep in the lowering dark. It was a long while before he slept. And before he slept he knew what he would do.

It was dawn when Marta shook him. She stood over him, milk pail in her hand and the three-legged milk stool clutched under her other arm.

"Get up," she said, her voice not like Marta's. "So this is where you are all night. You found Jon Arrow's barn! So you know now that Drushella will see him. And you will get up now and do the milking after all." She set the stool down, and walked away into the gray, thin dawn.

Giede felt his hands tightening again. He looked down at

them. And then he remembered what it was that he meant to do. He pulled himself up and went to the milking.

He could think of nothing all day but the fence sneaking across the far hills and the dancing that would be tonight. He missed Drushella and guessed that she had gone to her loft room to dress herself for Jon Arrow. Toward evening Giede's hands were never still, but tightening like iron until they ached, and the muscles in his shoulders were like hard leather. When Marta had cleared away the supper he sat by the empty fireplace, his pipe his only peace; Marta did not speak. When he could stand it no longer he got up, tapped the pipe clean, and went out to the front gate to wait for Jon Arrow. The boy would get no further than the gate, and Giede's heart thudded with a sharpness he had not known in all his life before.

And then coming with the dust he saw Jon Arrow's team. The small buggy was rolling fast, the swift grays one with the cloud of dust; after a time he could make out the man's purple neckerchief and his wide white hat.

Arrow swung the horses around to the narrow gate, said, "Howdy, Mr. Petrie," barely touching the hat that Giede could see now was soft as velvet. A smile set Arrow's sun wrinkles deep around his eyes. "A fine evening, sir."

Giede didn't answer, but rested his boot on the bottom rail of the fence.

"I'm Jon Arrow. We came across each other before." He had swung to the ground and was tying the team.

Giede said, "Don't do that."

Arrow looked up.

"You're not taking my girl dancing if that's what you're planning."

There was no smile on Arrow's face now. "That's what I'm planning."

"Drushella don't dance." Giede was trying his best to keep his voice calm while his hands were working the way they had been shutting and opening all day.

"I'll teach her to dance." Arrow's smile began, but Giede

moved close and Jon said, "I'm sorry if you don't like me. But you can't keep a girl shut."

Giede's fist caught him under the chin, a blow so sudden and hard that Jon staggered back against one of the grays. The horses reared and Jon, paying no attention to Giede, sawed them to quiet. When the horses stood he rubbed a quieting hand over the neck of the nearest one.

"There, fellow. You and Mr. Petrie got excited at the same time." He turned to Giede. "No need to get wrought up," he said, "you or the team."

The very evenness of his voice angered Giede. "There's need all right. You can turn your team around and go back to your valley and your—your barn." He choked on the word, moving in again to Arrow. "D'you hear?"

Jon took off his white hat, and Giede saw how his hands bit into it. "We're not going to have any trouble, Mr. Petrie. I asked Drushella to come to my barn dancing and she said she'd like to come and I'm taking her. So excuse me while I knock on your door." It was almost as if he said, "Excuse me while I knock you down."

Giede stood in the gateway. "Untie that team."

The smile was slipping back across Arrow's face. "They stand as quiet, whether they're tied or not." He put a hand on the fence rail and vaulted over, leaving Giede to watch helplessly while he strode up the path.

Drushella came out looking like a picture, the yellow cashmere held little-girl fashion above her ankles, as if she intended to skip rope. Giede winced. Coming down the path the full skirts swung wide, brushing against Jon Arrow's boots, and Drushella's hair, smooth around her head as spun brass, held Marta's fine shell comb tucked high. Giede felt smothered at the sight of the two walking there.

When they had almost reached him he faced around. "You're not going, Dru."

She half stopped. Then she caught her shawl closer across her bosom. "Of course I'm going, Pa. Don't be stupid. After all, it's only a barn dance." She and the boy kept coming on.

Her quick smile caught at Giede and he knew she thought he would let them pass. Before he could guess her intent she ran to him, took his face between her hands. He felt the softness of them. "Goodnight," she said, and kissed him on the forehead. Then she had passed him and Jon Arrow was helping her into the buggy.

Arrow caught up the reins and jumped in beside her. She waved. "Goodnight, Pa," she called back. Giede stood, watching the dust they made. Then he went in to Marta.

She was standing there, looking out the window. She turned as he slammed shut the door. Of course she had seen how it was that Drushella had wheedled him, and he felt a dull shame.

"She looks beautiful," Marta said, her voice gentle. There were tears on her wrinkled cheeks. These Giede had never seen but once before and that when he had been away at the lambing, out in the snow, and had come in to find her with the new, tiny Drushella at her breast. Then the tears had made him drop down beside her, ashamed as he was ashamed now. But she must not know this time how he felt.

"I said she was not to go dancing. Now she has gone. Things will never be the same again, Marta."

She heard the bitterness. "You mean you will never have her—us—alone to yourself anymore! You mean we will see beyond these mountains where there is something besides sunrise and sunset and working; and where there are sounds that sheep don't make—something besides bleating, and little bells tinkling. Where there is not forever a lambing to do, with the sick ones by the hearth, whining for their mas. You mean—"

"Lambing comes once a year," he said, anger running through him. "And there are never many sick ones to tend."

The practicality of it infuriated her. "You, Giede, had best wake up." She went to the kitchen and when he could hear her beating the biscuits that they would have for morning, he dropped wearily down in his rocking chair by the empty fireplace and watched the evening dull to night. When she came back into the room she seemed not to notice him. She lit the lamp and carried it past him into their small bedroom and after a while the light of it ceased to shine through the narrow crack below the door.

He got up then, and went toward the barn. It was time to be about the thing he meant to do.

He reached for the lantern on its nail. The cayuse nickered softly and he went to the animal, comforted a little by the cool, gentle nuzzling of the pony's nose. "We've got a job, cayuse, you and me." He struck a match to the lantern, then stood considering whether this was the thing he really wanted to do. The blanket in the corner where he had slept after his anger of yesterday—he had not folded it up; the saddles shining, the way Marta kept them; the three-legged milk stool she had put down so quietly when she said, "So you found the barn. So you know Drushella will see Jon Arrow. And you will get up and do the milking." What was it that had happened to Marta? To Dru?

He reached for a saddle, fresh anger flooding him, and tossed it to the pony's back, tightened the girth unmercifully, surprising Freckles into shying in protest and snorting so that Giede had to quiet him before he could lead him out. "You hush! You wake Marta with your noise and where will Giede be?" He swung into the saddle, feeling like an old man.

There was plenty of time for thinking, with the night sky staring down, and he stared back at it, fury driving him. He couldn't stop his anger, and he didn't want to. The hills slipped past, the stars dimmed a little with the slender moon. He rounded the hills into Yonder Valley and after a while he could hear the quick tempo of fiddle music and the pounding of men's boots and the voice of a caller, "Take your dosey-dos!" Giede thought, waiting for a sight of the lighted barn, *I'll take my dosey-dos.* The hand on the pony's rein was hard and steady; the other balanced his long rifle.

The barn came into view. He drew up, making out the dancers, and Drushella was the brightest streak of color in the light from the lanterns. Her yellow cashmere blotted out all of the other figures for Giede. Men caught her in their arms, spun her, let her go, turning her again and again until Giede felt dizzy with the hurt of it. When Jon Arrow came to her, whirled her to him, looking down at her, Giede's hands moved along the gun. But he could not stop his watching.

The fiddles broke off. The silence they left eased his dizziness, and quietly he urged the pony forward. It might be that Arrow would come outside now, and Giede would be ready. Then he saw Jon move toward the doorway, Drushella at his side.

They stood silhouetted against the lantern light, Jon's dark head bent above her shining one. They were talking, but there was only silence to wrap Giede close while iron fingers caught at his belly. Suddenly Drushella's laughter broke like music, cutting at Giede with a sound he never had heard before. He could not remember when she had been happy enough to laugh so, and now this Jon, this man that he hated and who stood so near her in the dark, could make her laugh.

Giede was trembling, feeling the night sky around him, and the silence. He stared at them and he thought, *When he touches her I will kill him.* But Jon did not touch her. *Make her laugh again. Only once. Please. Make her laugh again.* Then it came, so softly this time that he had to strain to hear it. Arrow's face bent close to hers, making the laughter tender and the gun in Giede's hand turned heavy. There was only silence after that, and the sight of the dark head bent to Drushella.

Giede looked away. He looked at the hills silvered with moonlight, and out across the wide, fine land and he saw the land as he never had seen it. He saw the fence that crept up until it disappeared in shadow. He saw the valley thickening with people and the pines cut away for building of cabins; and he heard laughter and saw Drushella's happiness. He heard her laughter echoing across other valleys where someday younger voices would take it up, carry it beyond far hills. And in its sound he heard his own name and Marta's.

The fiddles began again. But the two silhouetted figures stood quiet in the moonlight. Giede laid his rifle across his knees, feeling suddenly weak, but strong, too. And he faced his pony back into the night.

THE OUTSIDER

JUANITA BROOKS (1898–)

Born of pioneering Mormon stock in Bunkerville, Nevada, Juanita Brooks has gained a reputation as a distinguished historian of the West. Her book *The Mountain Meadows Massacre* (1950) has become a classic in the field. "The Outsider" is taken from her autobiography, *Quicksand and Cactus* (1982). It is a simply and poignantly written account of a young girl's first encounter with the larger world when an outsider stays briefly at her family's home in a small, isolated Mormon community.

He came in on the mail rig from Moapa. Pa stopped at the house just long enough to set his suitcase on the porch and tell Ma that he might be here for two nights, depending on whether he got done the things he had come to do. He was an Outsider, Pa said, but he seemed very nice and she needn't worry; he'd make some contacts uptown and likely be back in an hour or so.

An Outsider! I had never visited with one before in all my life. Most of our visitors were relatives who came in wagons from Mesquite. Those who came representing the Church leaders in St. George always stayed at the bishop's home and spoke to the people in meeting, reminding us of our part in the great plan of establishing the Kingdom of God upon the earth and making the desert blossom. They always praised our efforts. Even the drummers, who came to sell things at the store, were from ZCMI in Salt Lake City, and Church men also. And the trustees wouldn't think of hiring a teacher

who wasn't a member of the Church or who didn't keep the
Word of Wisdom.

What would an Outsider want in our town? What was he
here for, anyway? At our family prayers each morning both
Pa and Ma (when it was their turn—the older children shared
in this, too) always asked God to remember the missionaries
who were abroad preaching the Gospel to those who sat in
darkness. While this might be only figurative, I had somehow
the idea that all Outsiders would be underprivileged.

Ma was a little troubled at having to entertain him. We
weren't set up to run a hotel; we had enough children to fill
our house. But she marshaled all hands to help, one to clean
the washdish outside the kitchen door on the back porch,
wipe off the splashings from the oilcloth behind it, and put a
fresh towel in the roller; another to carry fresh ashes and a
new catalog to the outhouse and clean it out. She would
change the sheets on our bed upstairs, pick up our things, and
arrange them. I swept the front porch and dusted the living
room.

I had hardly finished when the Outsider came. Instantly I
sensed that there was something different about him, even
more than that he was wearing a suit and tie on a weekday.
Sitting in darkness, indeed! He seemed so vibrant and alive
that just standing there, he made things seem different.
Could he have a drink of water, please? I ran to get it.

As I handed the cup to him, I noticed how soft and white
his hands were, with the half-moon showing clearly on his
fingernails and no dirt under the nails. He sipped at the glass
gingerly. This was clearly not his first taste of the Virgin River
water. Noticing my interest, he asked, "Is it all like this?"

"Yes," I said. "Only that out of barrels is worse. We don't
mind it, but strangers always say that it tastes like a dose of
Epsom salts."

"A good comparison," he admitted, then added gener-
ously, "but this really *is* better." And he drank it quickly as an
ordeal to get through.

It was still not sundown. If I would direct him to the home

of some of my grandfather's descendants by his Indian wife, he would appreciate it very much. He was representing an Eastern university where people of Indian extraction could get a free education, he explained. So I pointed out the house where Aunt Annie lived, just one block south, and Aunt Janet in the other direction about three blocks away.

So that was why he was here! I told Ma, and together we wondered how much he had learned from Pa on the trip over, but he evidently did know about Grandpa's five wives, and that one of them was an Indian girl. Pa likely wouldn't go into any detail of how Grandpa had come to marry this girl, or what it had meant to the rest of the family to have Grandpa referred to by some of the uppity-ups as a "squaw man." We had all been trained to call all of the wives Grandma.

Now here was this Outsider come to offer these children a very special opportunity not open to any of the rest of us. Some of the older grandchildren were already married, but others just might be interested. In any event, the fact that we knew what the Outsider was in town for cleared the air for us all.

Before long he was back. Ma showed him where he would sleep, and the toilet facilities, and told him to make himself at home. He seemed to sense that we would be more comfortable if he spent his time in the front room, so that is what he did, moving about it easily and casually as if he appreciated our efforts to have it attractive. He looked at the organ with its latticework and its display of nicknacks, with my one boughten valentine in the center, and then sat down to it briefly and sounded out a few chords and ran a bit of melody with his right hand—not much, to be sure, but enough to show that he could play if he wanted to. I was so proud of that organ. There was only one other in the whole town, so when the Outsider said that it had a fine tone, I felt that he had paid a very special compliment. With him in it, the room did not look so grand as when our Mesquite relatives visited, though the organ did help to redeem it.

At supper he met all the children, repeated our names, and remembered them. He ate our homemade bread and new milk, with the extras of molasses and preserves and butter and cheese, as though he enjoyed it, except that he paused a little on the milk at first. Ma always apologized if she had to serve morning's milk, even though the cellar kept it quite cool. She thought that fresh milk was much more healthful and palatable; it was the way everyone else did, besides.

The Outsider made talk for us all, asking what grades we were in at school, and what we liked to do. He mentioned that on the way over the mesa today he had seen his first mirage, and told how real the lake and trees and buildings looked, which led to our story of the Davidsons, who had died of thirst about there, and of the dangers of mirages in general. He mentioned that he had traveled in Mexico and South America, but had never before ridden over a desert stretch such as this. This gave the little boys a chance to tell him about Old Griz and how Pa had found him out there, just about dead, and everyone got into the conversation until it seemed almost like a party.

When Ma thought the younger ones should go to bed, he suggested that maybe we could have a little picture show first. So with just a bit of adjusting of the lamp and some clever use of his hands, he made shadow pictures on the whitewashed wall. With a running commentary, he gave such an interesting program that no one wanted him to stop, not even Pa.

After the younger ones had gone to bed and things were cleared away a bit, Ma said she thought she would go to the dance. The Outsider said he would like to look in on it too, if there were no objection.

While we got ready, the Outsider sat in the front room reading. Ma had hopefully set the Bible and the Book of Mormon out on the stand and two or three tracts explaining our faith. Whether he looked at them was not so important to her as whether she did her duty by making them available. In the meantime, Pa had gone out to the corral to check on the animals and to see that things were generally in order before he went to bed.

On this night I took special pains with my shoes, blacking even the heels, and using two stovelids of soot in the process —the back lids near the stovepipe, which were always best. I touched up my hair with a bit of butter and rubbed some talcum on my face with a flannel cloth. I would pinch my cheeks a little just before we got there to make them red.

The crowd was all gathered and the dance ready to begin when we got there. The benches had been pushed back around the walls, with the surplus ones stacked on the back of the stage. The lamps were all cleaned and filled, the tin reflectors behind them polished. The girls sat demurely on one side of the room and the boys on the other, while a few couples who were going steady stood together near the door. The Outsider did not know the rules of our dances, for he came along with us and sat on the women's side of the hall— our men would have dropped dead before one of them would have done that! But the doorkeeper had accepted his fifty cents without giving him a ticket, so that he could sit where he pleased.

Ma certainly did enjoy the dances. Besides the music and the activity, there was the chance to visit with other women, to note the new dresses and decide whether they were homemade or had come from Montgomery Ward or Bellas Hess. She had noticed who danced with whom, and how, and sometimes discovered a budding romance before the people were conscious of it themselves. She often held a baby while its younger mother shook off her cares in the wide whirlings of a quadrille, or she exchanged experiences with one in a shapeless "mother hubbard" who couldn't dance herself, but came along while her husband did. There was an unwritten rule that so long as he sat out the first and last dance beside his pregnant wife, a young man might dance as much as he cared to.

So on this night I sat between Ma and the Outsider, who was on the end of the bench near the stage. The musician, his hat pulled low over his eyes to protect them from the glare, was absentmindedly pulling his accordion in and out in long, windy chords, as though he were tuning it up.

The floor manager stepped to the center front.

"Give us your attention, please, and we will begin this dance. Brother Bunker, will you offer the opening prayer?"

"Friends, Romans, countrymen, lend me your ears!" the Outsider said *sotto voce* to me. As Brother Bunker came forward, he offered the stock petition for such occasions, asking God to help us all to enjoy ourselves in wholesome recreation, and praying that no accident or evil might mar the activities.

"Fill up the floor for a waltz," the floor manager next called out.

The boys all hurried across the hall for their partners, and all promenaded arm in arm in a grand march until the floor manager gave the signal. This first waltz was precious and prolonged. Watching the musician, the Outsider imitated the jerky movement of the accordion and said, "Link-ed sweet-ness l-o-n-g drawn out."

It was as if he had shared with me a delicious tidbit. I knew that he did not make these up; he had found them in books.

As the dance went on, the men had to dance in turns and by numbers, either odds and evens or numbers one to twenty-four and twenty-four to forty-eight. Each dance was repeated so that no one was cheated. Ambitious young men who wished to dance every time must either buy two tickets, or perhaps borrow one from an older man who would sit his out.

The calling of the dance was important in the selection of a partner, for one who could waltz well might become confused in a quadrille, and another who could do the one-two-three-kick of the schottische would be like a cow-in-tow on the polka. At the end of each dance the young man accompanied his lady to her seat and then returned to his own side of the hall.

Through it all the floor manager moved among the crowd,

not dancing himself but seeing that none of the boys should "wring on" or get too rowdy, and keeping his eye on the conditions in general. Meanwhile the Outsider seemed mildly amused at the gusto with which the young men stamped and whirled and swung their partners.

During the intermission the floor was swept, two boys pushing the dirt ahead of them in a long windrow. A few couples walked out during this process, but most of the people remained in their places. The floor manager walked back and forth behind the sweepers, whittling off a candle and scattering the shavings. Someone called from the sidelines for a step dance by Uncle Tom and Aunt Lene.

"Uncle Tom and Aunt Lene will do a double-shuffle," the manager called out without stopping his knife.

Uncle Tom was tall and angular; Aunt Lene was short and plump. Both had great-grandchildren, so should have given up dancing long ago, yet they came promptly to the center of the hall and faced each other. The accordion started, lively, staccato. They waited for the exact note, bowed deeply to each other, and began. Holding her skirt up slightly with one hand, Aunt Lene swayed gently as her feet did little shuttle steps in and out under the hem. Uncle Tom gyrated in a circle around her, one foot shuffling forward, the other kicking outward, one arm close at his side, the other flapping loosely in time with the kicking foot—the whole not unlike the preenings of an amorous turkey cock. There was a double figure eight, where they passed back to back in the middle of it; there were intricate cuttings in and out, until at the end, when they faced each other again and bowed.

The Outsider clapped and clapped, and even stamped his feet in approval too, as some of the others were doing. "Come and trip it as you go, on the light, fantastic toe," he said. "Truly a *fantastic* toe!" Then when the floor manager shouted for everyone to fill up the floor again, he said right out loud, "On with the dance! Let joy be unconfined!"

I was so thrilled to see how he entered into the spirit of the party. I knew that he was saying things out of books again, but such appropriate things! Such unusual things! Surely he was not one who had been sitting in darkness, and whatever light he had I wanted some of.

At last it was time for the "Home, Sweet Home" waltz. Some of the married folks just waltzed as far as the door and went right on out so they'd not have to wait through the closing prayer. Others danced around once or twice before they escaped, so that by the time it was half done there was plenty of room on the floor.

The Outsider turned to me. "Would you like to try this one?"

Would I! I who had not danced at a grown-up dance in my life, would I like to dance with him, the best-dressed and handsomest man there! I stood up, but my heartbeat nearly deafened me. As we started, I looked down, because I didn't know where else to look.

"Don't watch your feet," he said softly. "Hold your head up. Listen to the music. Get the feel of it, and your feet will take care of themselves."

I did, and it worked. We went all the way around the hall twice without breaking step once, as though just by his skill he carried me along. I could not talk; I had nothing to say. He hummed the tune and kept his head up too, above mine.

As we started back to where Ma was still standing and visiting, I said, a little breathlessly, "Thank you. That was a new experience for me."

For a second he saw me. Then he quoted again: "All experience is an arch wherethro' Gleams that untravell'd world whose margin fades for ever and for ever when I move." He stopped as if at a loss to go on, then added, "You know. That *untravell'd* world."

We had stopped. His hand was on my arm just above the elbow, and I leaned against him just the least bit, hardly conscious that the doorkeeper had closed the door and was standing in front of it, that the floor manager had called on Brother Jones to say the closing prayer, and that Brother Jones had asked the crowd to "Please arise, and we will be dismissed." I stood with bowed head, not heeding the prayer but with "that untravell'd world whose margin fades for ever and for ever when I move" saying itself through my mind.

With the Amen, the door was opened and the general leave-taking made any further talk impossible. Outside I walked on one side of Ma, the Outsider on the other, down the road. He asked about the musician and about Uncle Tom and Aunt Lene, so that Ma had a good time explaining how things were in our town, even the using of the meetinghouse for the dance. Ma invited him to go to Sunday School, but he excused himself, saying that he had an early morning appointment that would prevent it.

Ma served breakfast to him and Pa by themselves the next morning while we were doing the chores. I guessed that he had met with no success in Aunt Annie's family, or any of the others. They did not want to be classed as Indians. They were not Indians; they were descendants of Dudley Leavitt, born under the Covenant and with special blessings already promised.

When I came in from Sunday School, he was gone. He had found a way back to Moapa with someone who was going, and he would get there in time to catch the night train, which would save a full day. My heart was like lead. I had thought that I would see him at dinner, at least, when we would have an ironed tablecloth on and Ma was serving chicken and noodles, her very best dish.

That afternoon I took the mail ponies down to the pasture and rode Selah back, coming by the hill road. It was just past sundown, so I rode to the top of my favorite knoll, where I could see far in every direction. At the west, the mesa stretched endlessly, pink in the reflection of the evening light.

Out into the vivid sunset the Outsider had gone to Moapa. Where would he go from there? I realized that while he knew a great deal about me, I knew almost nothing about him, not even his name. I looked over my world here on the edge of the desert, its sun-blistered miles of rock and clay—a barren world, full of emptiness. I knew that there were places where grass and trees and flowers grew just for the fun of it, without having to be nursed along by irrigation. "That untravell'd world whose margin fades for ever and for ever when I move," I said to myself. Did that mean like chasing the end of the rainbow? Or like going off the road to find the greenery and water of a mirage? Or was it not the physical world at all to which the Outsider referred—but the world of thought, of knowledge?

So sitting astride my dappled pony, my bonnet on my shoulders, my braids undone, I studied this out and determined that I would see some of the world beyond the desert, that I would go to a college or a university or whatever it was that one went to in order to learn of books, and how to talk like books. I would not wait for life to come to me; I would go out to meet it.

As I watched the glory in the west bloom to such brilliance that it almost hurt to see it, and then begin to fade, it seemed almost like the bright spot which he had made in my life. Maybe when I was all grown up and out in the great world, just *maybe* I would meet the Outsider there, and I would be so changed that he would not know me. But I would tell him, and then he would remember. Just like a storybook.

YELLOW WOMAN
LESLIE SILKO (1948-)

The poet, short story writer, and novelist Leslie Silko was born in Albuquerque, New Mexico. She has written about herself: "I grew up at Laguna Pueblo. I am of mixed-breed ancestry, but what I know is Laguna. This place I am from is everything I am as a writer and human being." The only American Indian author represented in this anthology, Silko draws timeless portraits of Indian family life. "Yellow Woman," first collected in *The Man to Send Rain Clouds* (1974), demonstrates her ability to weave an ancient Indian myth into a contemporary setting. The characters are haunting: the female narrator; Silva, her abductor; and the narrator's grandfather, whose spirit unites the narrator with her ancestral past.

ONE

My thigh clung to his with dampness, and I watched the sun rising up through the tamaracks and willows. The small brown water birds came to the river and hopped across the mud, leaving brown scratches in the alkali-white crust. They bathed in the river silently. I could hear the water, almost at our feet where the narrow fast channel bubbled and washed green ragged moss and fern leaves. I looked at him beside me, rolled in the red blanket on the white river sand. I cleaned the sand out of the cracks between my toes, squinting because the sun was above the willow trees. I looked at him for the last time, sleeping on the white river sand.

I felt hungry and followed the river south the way we had come the afternoon before, following our footprints that were already blurred by lizard tracks and bug trails. The horses were still lying down, and the black one whinnied when he saw me but he did not get up—maybe it was because the corral was made out of thick cedar branches and the horses had not yet felt the sun like I had. I tried to look beyond the pale red mesas to the pueblo. I knew it was there, even if I could not see it, on the sandrock hill above the river, the same river that moved past me now and had reflected the moon last night.

The horse felt warm underneath me. He shook his head and pawed the sand. The bay whinnied and leaned against the gate trying to follow, and I remembered him asleep in the red blanket beside the river. I slid off the horse and tied him close to the other horse. I walked north with the river again, and the white sand broke loose in footprints over footprints.

"Wake up."

He moved in the blanket and turned his face to me with his eyes still closed. I knelt down to touch him.

"I'm leaving."

He smiled now, eyes still closed. "You are coming with me, remember?" He sat up now with his bare dark chest and belly in the sun.

"Where?"

"To my place."

"And will I come back?"

He pulled his pants on. I walked away from him, feeling him behind me and smelling the willows.

"Yellow Woman," he said.

I turned to face him. "Who are you?" I asked.

He laughed and knelt on the low, sandy bank, washing his face in the river. "Last night you guessed my name, and you knew why I had come."

I stared past him at the shallow moving water and tried to remember the night, but I could only see the moon in the water and remember his warmth around me.

"But I only said that you were him and that I was Yellow

Woman—I'm not really her—I have my own name and I come from the pueblo on the other side of the mesa. Your name is Silva and you are a stranger I met by the river yesterday afternoon."

He laughed softly. "What happened yesterday has nothing to do with what you will do today, Yellow Woman."

"I know—that's what I'm saying—the old stories about the ka'tsina spirit and Yellow Woman can't mean us."

My old grandpa liked to tell those stories best. There is one about Badger and Coyote, who went hunting and were gone all day, and when the sun was going down they found a house. There was a girl living there alone, and she had light hair and eyes and she told them that they could sleep with her. Coyote wanted to be with her all night so he sent Badger into a prairie-dog hole, telling him he thought he saw something in it. As soon as Badger crawled in, Coyote blocked up the entrance with rocks and hurried back to Yellow Woman.

"Come here," he said gently.

He touched my neck and I moved close to him to feel his breathing and to hear his heart. I was wondering if Yellow Woman had known who she was—if she knew that she would become part of the stories. Maybe she'd had another name that her husband and relatives called her so that only the ka'tsina from the north and the storytellers would know her as Yellow Woman. But I didn't go on; I felt him all around me, pushing me down into the white river sand.

Yellow Woman went away with the spirit from the north and lived with him and his relatives. She was gone for a long time, but then one day she came back and she brought twin boys.

"Do you know the story?"

"What story?" He smiled and pulled me close to him as he said this. I was afraid lying there on the red blanket. All I could know was the way he felt, warm, damp, his body beside me. This is the way it happens in the stories, I was thinking, with no thought beyond the moment she meets the ka'tsina spirit and they go.

"I don't have to go. What they tell in stories was real only then, back in time immemorial, like they say."

He stood up and pointed at my clothes tangled in the blanket. "Let's go," he said.

I walked beside him, breathing hard because he walked fast, his hand around my wrist. I had stopped trying to pull away from him, because his hand felt cool and the sun was high, drying the river bed into alkali. I will see someone, eventually I will see someone, and then I will be certain that he is only a man—some man from nearby—and I will be sure that I am not Yellow Woman. Because she is from out of time past and I live now and I've been to school and there are highways and pickup trucks that Yellow Woman never saw.

It was an easy ride north on horseback. I watched the change from the cottonwood trees along the river to the junipers that brushed past us in the foothills, and finally there were only piñons, and when I looked up at the rim of the mountain plateau I could see pine trees growing on the edge. Once I stopped to look down, but the pale sandstone had disappeared and the river was gone and the dark lava hills were all around. He touched my hand, not speaking, but always singing softly a mountain song and looking into my eyes.

I felt hungry and wondered what they were doing at home now—my mother, my grandmother, my husband, and the baby. Cooking breakfast, saying, "Where did she go?—maybe kidnaped," and Al going to the tribal police with the details: "She went walking along the river."

The house was made with black lava rock and red mud. It was high above the spreading miles of arroyos and long mesas. I smelled a mountain smell of pitch and buck brush. I stood there beside the black horse, looking down on the small, dim country we had passed, and I shivered.

"Yellow Woman, come inside where it's warm."

TWO

He lit a fire in the stove. It was an old stove with a round
belly and an enamel coffeepot on top. There was only the
stove, some faded Navajo blankets, and a bedroll and cardboard box. The floor was made of smooth adobe plaster, and
there was one small window facing east. He pointed at the
box.

"There's some potatoes and the frying pan." He sat on the
floor with his arms around his knees pulling them close to his
chest and he watched me fry the potatoes. I didn't mind him
watching me because he was always watching me—he had
been watching me since I came upon him sitting on the
riverbank trimming leaves from a willow twig with his knife.
We ate from the pan and he wiped the grease from his fingers
on his Levi's.

"Have you brought women here before?" He smiled and
kept chewing, so I said, "Do you always use the same tricks?"

"What tricks?" He looked at me like he didn't understand.

"The story about being a ka'tsina from the mountains. The
story about Yellow Woman."

Silva was silent; his face was calm.

"I don't believe it. Those stories couldn't happen now," I
said.

He shook his head and said softly, "But someday they will
talk about us, and they will say, 'Those two lived long ago
when things like that happened.' "

He stood up and went out. I ate the rest of the potatoes and
thought about things—about the noise the stove was making
and the sound of the mountain wind outside. I remembered
yesterday and the day before, and then I went outside.

I walked past the corral to the edge where the narrow trail
cut through the black rimrock. I was standing in the sky with
nothing around me but the wind that came down from the
blue mountain peak behind me. I could see faint mountain
images in the distance miles across the vast spread of mesas

and valleys and plains. I wondered who was over there to feel the mountain wind on those sheer blue edges—who walked on the pine needles in those blue mountains.

"Can you see the pueblo?" Silva was standing behind me. I shook my head. "We're too far away."

"From here I can see the world." He stepped out on the edge. "The Navajo reservation begins over there." He pointed to the east. "The Pueblo boundaries are over here." He looked below us to the south, where the narrow trail seemed to come from. "The Texans have their ranches over there, starting with that valley, the Concho Valley. The Mexicans run some cattle over there too."

"Do you ever work for them?"

"I steal from them," Silva answered. The sun was dropping behind us and shadows were filling the land below. I turned away from the edge that dropped forever into the valleys below.

"I'm cold," I said; "I'm going inside." I started wondering about this man who could speak the Pueblo language so well but who lived on a mountain and rustled cattle. I decided that this man Silva must be Navajo, because Pueblo men didn't do things like that.

"You must be a Navajo."

Silva shook his head gently. "Little Yellow Woman," he said, "you never give up, do you? I have told you who I am. The Navajo people know me, too." He knelt down and unrolled the bedroll and spread the extra blankets out on a piece of canvas. The sun was down, and the only light in the house came from outside—the dim orange light from sundown.

I stood there and waited for him to crawl under the blankets.

"What are you waiting for?" he said, and I lay down beside him. He undressed me slowly like the night before beside the river—kissing my face gently and running his hands up and down my belly and legs. He took off my pants and then he laughed.

"Why are you laughing?"

"You are breathing so hard."

I pulled away from him and turned my back to him.

He pulled me around and pinned me down with his arms and chest. "You don't understand, do you, little Yellow Woman? You will do what I want."

And again he was all around me with his skin slippery against mine, and I was afraid because I understood that his strength could hurt me. I lay underneath him and I knew that he could destroy me. But later, while he slept beside me, I touched his face and I had a feeling—the kind of feeling for him that overcame me that morning along the river. I kissed him on the forehead and he reached out for me.

When I woke up in the morning he was gone. It gave me a strange feeling, because for a long time I sat there on the blankets and looked around the little house for some object of his—some proof that he had been there or maybe that he was coming back. Only the blankets and the cardboard box remained. The .30–30 that had been leaning in the corner was gone, and so was the knife I had used the night before. He was gone, and I had my chance to go now. But first I had to eat, because I knew it would be a long walk home.

I found some dried apricots in the cardboard box, and I sat down on a rock at the edge of the plateau rim. There was no wind and the sun warmed me. I was surrounded by silence. I drowsed with apricots in my mouth, and I didn't believe that there were highways or railroads or cattle to steal.

When I woke up, I stared down at my feet in the black mountain dirt. Little black ants were swarming over the pine needles around my foot. They must have smelled the apricots. I thought about my family far below me. They would be wondering about me because this had never happened to me before. The tribal police would file a report. But if old Grandpa weren't dead he would tell them what happened—he would laugh and say, "Stolen by a ka'tsina, a mountain spirit. She'll come home—they usually do." There are enough of them to handle things. My mother and grandmother will raise the baby like they raised me. Al will find someone else, and they will go on like before, except that there will be a story about the day I disappeared while I was walking along the river. Silva had come for me; he said he had. I did not decide to go. I just went. Moonflowers blossom in the sandhills before dawn, just as I followed him. That's what I was thinking as I wandered along the trail through the pine trees.

It was noon when I got back. When I saw the stone house I remembered that I had meant to go home. But that didn't seem important anymore, maybe because there were little blue flowers growing in the meadow behind the stone house and the gray squirrels were playing in the pines next to the house. The horses were standing in the corral, and there was a beef carcass hanging on the shady side of a big pine in front of the house. Flies buzzed around the clotted blood that hung from the carcass. Silva was washing his hands in a bucket full of water. He must have heard me coming because he spoke to me without turning to face me.

"I've been waiting for you."

"I went walking in the big pine trees."

I looked into the bucket full of bloody water with brown-and-white animal hairs floating in it. Silva stood there letting his hand drip, examining me intently.

"Are you coming with me?"

"Where?" I asked him.

"To sell the meat in Marquez."

"If you're sure it's O.K."

"I wouldn't ask you if it wasn't," he answered.

He sloshed the water around in the bucket before he dumped it out and set the bucket upside down near the door. I followed him to the corral and watched him saddle the horses. Even beside the horses he looked tall, and I asked him again if he wasn't Navajo. He didn't say anything; he just shook his head and kept cinching up the saddle.

"But Navajos are tall."

"Get on the horse," he said, "and let's go."

The last thing he did before we started down the steep trail was to grab the .30–30 from the corner. He slid the rifle into the scabbard that hung from his saddle.

"Do they ever try to catch you?" I asked.

"They don't know who I am."

"Then why did you bring the rifle?"

"Because we are going to Marquez, where the Mexicans live."

THREE

The trail leveled out on a narrow ridge that was steep on both sides like an animal spine. On one side I could see where the trail went around the rocky gray hills and disappeared into the southeast where the pale sandrock mesas stood in the distance near my home. On the other side was a trail that went west, and as I looked far into the distance I thought I saw the little town. But Silva said no, that I was looking in the wrong place, that I just thought I saw houses. After that I quit looking off into the distance; it was hot and the wildflowers were closing up their deep yellow petals. Only the waxy cactus flowers bloomed in the bright sun, and I saw every color that a cactus blossom can be; the white ones and the red ones were still buds, but the purple and the yellow were blossoms, open full and the most beautiful of all.

Silva saw him before I did. The white man was riding a big gray horse, coming up the trail toward us. He was traveling fast and the gray horse's feet sent rocks rolling off the trail into the dry tumbleweeds. Silva motioned for me to stop and we watched the white man. He didn't see us right away, but finally his horse whinnied at our horses and he stopped. He looked at us briefly before he loped the gray horse across the three hundred yards that separated us. He stopped his horse in front of Silva, and his young fat face was shadowed by the brim of his hat. He didn't look mad, but his small, pale eyes moved from the blood-soaked gunnysacks hanging from my saddle to Silva's face and then back to my face.

"Where did you get the fresh meat?" the white man asked.

"I've been hunting," Silva said, and when he shifted his weight in the saddle the leather creaked.

"The hell you have, Indian. You've been rustling cattle. We've been looking for the thief for a long time."

The rancher was fat, and sweat began to soak through his white cowboy shirt and the wet cloth stuck to the thick rolls of belly fat. He almost seemed to be panting from the exertion of talking, and he smelled rancid, maybe because Silva scared him.

Silva turned to me and smiled. "Go back up the mountain, Yellow Woman."

The white man got angry when he heard Silva speak in a language he couldn't understand. "Don't try anything, Indian. Just keep riding to Marquez. We'll call the state police from there."

The rancher must have been unarmed because he was very frightened and if he had a gun he would have pulled it out then. I turned my horse around and the rancher yelled, "Stop!" I looked at Silva for an instant and there was something ancient and dark—something I could feel in my stomach—in his eyes, and when I glanced at his hand I saw his finger on the trigger of the .30–30 that was still in the saddle scabbard. I slapped my horse across the flank and the sacks of raw meat swung against my knees as the horse leaped up the trail. It was hard to keep my balance, and once I thought I felt the saddle slipping backward; it was because of this that I could not look back.

I didn't stop until I reached the ridge where the trail forked. The horse was breathing deep gasps and there was a dark film of sweat on its neck. I looked down in the direction I had come from, but I couldn't see the place. I waited. The wind came up and pushed warm air past me. I looked up at the sky, pale blue and full of thin clouds and fading vapor trails left by jets.

I think four shots were fired—I remember hearing four hollow explosions that reminded me of deer hunting. There could have been more shots after that, but I couldn't have heard them because my horse was running again and the loose rocks were making too much noise as they scattered around his feet.

Horses have a hard time running downhill, but I went that way instead of uphill to the mountain because I thought it was safer. I felt better with the horse running southeast past the round gray hills that were covered with cedar trees and black lava rock. When I got to the plain in the distance I could see the dark green patches of tamaracks that grew along the river; and beyond the river I could see the beginning of the pale sandrock mesas. I stopped the horse and looked back to see if anyone was coming; then I got off the horse and turned the horse around, wondering if it would go back to its corral under the pines on the mountain. It looked back at me for a moment and then plucked a mouthful of green tumbleweeds before it trotted back up the trail with its ears pointed forward, carrying its head daintily to one side to avoid stepping on the dragging reins. When the horse disappeared over the last hill, the gunnysacks full of meat were still swinging and bouncing.

FOUR

I walked toward the river on a wood hauler's road that I knew would eventually lead to the paved road. I was thinking about waiting beside the road for someone to drive by, but by the time I got to the pavement I had decided it wasn't very far to walk if I followed the river back the way Silva and I had come.

The river water tasted good, and I sat in the shade under a cluster of silvery willows. I thought about Silva, and I felt sad at leaving him; still, there was something strange about him, and I tried to figure it out all the way back home.

I came back to the place on the riverbank where he had been sitting the first time I saw him. The green willow leaves that he had trimmed from the branch were still lying there, wilted in the sand. I saw the leaves and I wanted to go back to him—to kiss him and to touch him—but the mountains were too far away now. And I told myself, because I believe it, he will come back sometime and be waiting again by the river.

I followed the path up from the river into the village. The sun was getting low, and I could smell supper cooking when I got to the screen door of my house. I could hear their voices inside—my mother was telling my grandmother how to fix the Jell-O and my husband, Al, was playing with the baby. I decided to tell them that some Navajo had kidnaped me, but I was sorry that old Grandpa wasn't alive to hear my story because it was the Yellow Woman stories he liked to tell best.

Vicki Piekarski was coeditor-in-chief of the *Encyclopedia of Frontier and Western Fiction* and coauthor of *The Frontier Experience: A Reader's Guide to the Life and Literature of the American West.* She was associate editor and a contributor to the three-volume *Close-up on the Cinema* series published by Scarecrow Press; a contributor to *Twentieth-Century Western Writers;* and a reviewer of Western fiction for *The West Coast Review of Books.* She is on the adjunct faculty at Lewis and Clark College in Portland, Oregon.